THE SPECTACULAR KID

THE SPECTACULAR KID

Robert J. Horton

GUNSMOKE

First published in the UK by Hodder and Stoughton

This hardback edition 2011
by AudioGO Ltd
by arrangement with
Golden West Literary Agency

ISBN 978 1 445 85670 4

British Library Cataloguing in Publication Data available.

Printed and bound in Great Britain by
MPG Books Group Limited

CONTENTS

CHAPTER I
AN OBSERVER

Along a winding trail leading down from the higher slopes of Tenderfoot Divide a youth was riding. On either side the jack pines crowded to the edge of the dim path. In the occasional meadows the boy's big, iron-gray horse threw up its head and cantered eagerly, while the young man's cheery whistle broke in upon the whisper of the breeze in the timber. The crimson rays of the dying sun struck the silver trappings on the boy's bridle and gleamed red upon the ivory handle of the gun in the worn holster strapped to his right thigh.

Dark, slim of build, the youth rode with graceful abandon. The dreamy look in his eyes sharpened to a keen, searching gaze, as he looked ahead, when longer stretches of the trail were visible. He plainly was alert.

A thin, blue haze hung over the high hills; for it was midsummer. The breeze bore the scent of baked earth, of dry timber, of grasses ripened and sear. The little mountain streams had narrowed to ripples in the drought. Gradually the ridges became bathed in variegated colors, harbingers of the mountain twilight.

As he emerged from the forest into the rounded, sparsely timbered foothills, the youthful rider came upon a road, drove in his spurs and galloped along it. Half an hour later, as night was settling, he rode into the little town of Dry Crossing on Smith River.

He put his horse in the open shed behind the one gen-

7

eral store and entered by the rear door.

"Gimme some bacon an' beans," he ordered gayly, with a flashing smile for the young lady who was in charge.

"Any particular amount of 'em?" asked the girl with a toss of her head.

The boy took out tobacco and papers and began to fashion a cigarette. He grinned amiably.

"Gettin' time to light the lamps, ain't it?" he drawled. "You're worth lookin' at in a better light than this."

The girl answered his smile; then regarded him haughtily. "I don't reckon you figure on payin' for the bacon an' beans with compliments," she observed severely. "An' the lamps are too high for me to reach. Dad usually lights 'em on the stepladder."

The youth laughed delightedly. "Show me the ladder, an' I'll light 'em," he offered cheerily.

The girl's smile returned, after a moment of hesitation, and she pointed to a stepladder in the rear.

While the boy was lighting the hanging lamps, he called out his order for provisions. It wasn't a large order. The supplies could easily be carried in a slicker pack on the rear of his saddle.

"Seems to be quite a few of you young gents travelin' light these days," said the girl, as she wrapped the few packages.

The youth, who had been regarding her in open admiration, wrinkled his brow. "Meanin' there's more'n one of us?"

"Another fellow was in here a few minutes ago an' bought just about as much as you did," she said.

8

"What'd he look like?" asked the boy, idly curious.

"'Bout your size, only blond an' good looking," replied the girl with a tantalizing laugh. "Thought maybe you was pardners."

He disregarded her taunt and frowned. "I don't know everybody in these hills, ma'am," he said quietly; "fact is, I don't know hardly anybody on this west side of the Divide—an' I ain't got any pardner."

Something in the tone caused the girl to look at him quickly. She saw a baffling, wistful look in his eyes, caught a strange hint of forlornness in his manner.

"You'll get acquainted quick enough if you're around long," she said suddenly. "You're that kind."

A smile lit up his dark, handsome face; his teeth flashed white and even against the healthy tan.

"Sometimes I get acquainted too easy," he observed. "An' there is places, maybe, where I'm too dog-goned well known."

He left by the rear door, carrying his packages. In the shed he removed the yellow slicker from the rear of his saddle, wrapped his purchases in it, and replaced it. He led the big gray around the store and turned toward a building from which yellow shafts of light streaked across the dusty street.

Dropping his bridle reins he pushed through the swinging doors. With his entrance into the place the boy's eyes shone keen and challenging; his movements became extremely deliberate; a cool confidence seemed to radiate from him, and he was inordinately the personification of cheerfulness.

"A fine evening," he said, addressing no one in particular, but looking at a man who stood behind a bar which ranged along the right side of the room.

A penetrating quality in his voice brought looks from a number who were playing cards at tables to the left. A youth sitting at a small lunch counter in the rear turned and regarded him swiftly. A large man with a bristling two-day growth of beard drained a glass of white liquor and scowled at him.

"What'll you have?" asked the bartender, who evidently was searching his memory in a strenuous effort to identify the newcomer.

"Well, it's warm, an' I've been ridin' in the dust till my throat feels like a hot tamale. What'd you suggest under those circumstances?"

The bartender set out a bottle of white liquor, with a grin.

"I reckon you got me wrong," sang the boy cheerfully. "I'm aimin' to settle the dust in my throat, not to raise a cloud of it in my head."

The bartender frowned.

"Oh, give him milk," growled the big man, reaching for the bottle the youth had rejected.

"That wouldn't be so bad, if it was cold enough," drawled the boy, looking squarely into the big man's eyes. "You ever try it?" The question came sharp and clear.

The big man put down the bottle and swung about in angry surprise.

"You're talking right smart for a kid," he said, with a narrowing of his eyes.

"I'm smart enough to know this place has got something to sell besides mule liquor," the boy retorted. "An' I don't remember askin' you to order for me." Then, turning to the bartender: "Make me a cold lemonade outa lemons."

The flash of the silver ornaments about his person was reflected in the boy's eyes. The bartender turned quickly to follow instructions.

"I was thinking milk would match the color of that ivory-handled gun of yourn," sneered the big man.

"So it would," drawled the youth. There was a barely perceptible movement of his right arm, and his gun lay in his palm.

Spectators who had been watching with interest the amusing scene, gasped at the lightning rapidity of the draw.

"An' I'm thinkin' the color of its barrel might match your disposition," said the youth coolly, as he dropped the weapon into its holster.

"I've got you spotted now!" cried the bartender in excitement. "I thought you sized up to descriptions I heard. I know you!"

"Maybe so; but don't forget that lemonade," the boy cautioned.

"You're 'The Spectacular Kid!' " breathed the bartender.

At mention of the name the gaze of every man in the place became alert. There was utter silence, as the significance of the revelation of the strange youth's identity sank in. Here was a youthful gunman, brought up by an alleged outlaw and gambler—a killer, according to the story which had drifted through the hills to the people of the Smith River country.

But there was no doubting the menacing efficiency of that draw. The big man's gaze, keen and glittering, now was focused upon The Kid with peculiar intensity.

"If I'd known who you was, I might have offered to take one of them lemonades with you," he said finally, in a suave voice.

"Don't let that worry you," replied The Kid coldly. "I'm used to drinkin' alone."

Looking past the big man, The Kid saw the youth at the counter in the rear steal quickly out of the place by a back door. The big man continued to regard him thoughtfully, while The Kid drank his lemonade with scornful nonchalance. As The Kid paid his score and started for the door, the other leaned across the bar and engaged the bartender in whispered conversation.

The Kid swung into the saddle and spurred the big gray into the foothill road. He had learned what he had suspected. Throughout the high hills and the surrounding country he was branded as a gunman. He thought of the circumstances which had endowed him with this sinister reputation, and his face became grim.

On the crest of a high ridge he checked his horse and looked out over the vast, dim reaches of timbered slopes and towering peaks, ghastly white in the silver light of the moon. He listened.

Above the whine of vagrant winds in pine and fir, came the dull echoes of hoofs on the trail below. He shrugged and rode on to a secluded meadow under the main range of the Divide, where a small tent gleamed white against the dark background of forest.

CHAPTER II
THE POSSE

The Kid unsaddled and turned his horse out to graze upon the luscious grasses of the meadow. He hung the saddle from a branch of a pine, where it would be out of reach of porcupines, using his lariat. The slicker pack he put in the tent. Then he built a small fire and assembled cooking utensils and provisions for a meal.

At frequent intervals he paused in his tasks and listened. The meadow was a short distance back from the trail, but the blaze of his camp fire would be visible to any horseman riding toward the Divide. Only once after reaching his camp did he catch the sound of hoofs.

He went swiftly about the work of getting supper. His face appeared moody in the flickering light of the flames. Several times he walked into the shadows beyond the blaze of light and gazed up at the outlines of the Divide and the dark sea of sky alive with stars. He was sitting down to eat, when a man stepped noiselessly into the clearing, walked quickly within the rim of light about the camp fire, raised his hands, and stood looking at him.

"Put 'em down," said The Kid; "I was expectin' you."

The other—a youth about The Kid's size, blond, with sun-burned features, looked surprised.

"Expectin' me!" he blurted. "How's that?"

The Kid looked him over. He was the youth he had seen eating at the lunch counter in the resort in Dry Crossing. He suspected he was the same young fellow the girl in the store had mentioned.

"I dunno," said The Kid. "Guess the way you looked at me in that joint down below, an' the way you slid out, sort of impressed me that you'd be ridin' along. Don't suppose you're hungry?"

The other shook his head and looked around uneasily. Then he sat down, while The Kid attacked his meal with casual glances at him.

"I left my horse over in the timber," said the newcomer.

The Kid nodded.

"My name's Ben Marcy," the other volunteered. "I'd heard of The Spectacular Kid clear down where I come from."

The Kid showed interest. "Maybe you've sort of forgotten where that place is," he drawled. "I don't need to know."

"I'm from down Musselshell way," said Marcy with evident truthfulness.

The Kid glanced up quickly. "You've come aroun' by a long way," he observed.

Ben Marcy grinned. There was something catching about that grin, and The Kid smiled back.

"I hit along west," explained Ben, "until I came to the high-tension line. Then I followed the cleared-off space under the wires an' aroun' the towers in this direction. I traveled slow." He regarded The Kid wist-

14

fully. "I was herdin' some horses," he added after some hesitation.

The Kid didn't look at him. He was thinking hard. It might be that a posse would not think of following the cleared trail under the high-tension wires, which carries electrical power from the great power houses, at the falls of the Missouri, across the mountains to run the trains of a transcontinental railway over the Rockies. That power line ran through the pass above his camp. Marcy had doubtless left his horses cached and had ridden into Dry Crossing for urgently needed supplies.

Ben studied The Kid's face without being able to read his thoughts. Was The Kid an outlaw killer? What was it about The Kid's look and manner which had drawn him to him? Had he made a mistake in intruding upon The Kid's camp? Then The Kid spoke quietly.

"You're in the forest reserve now. All the grazin' privileges in here are taken by stockmen livin' in the hills an' ranchers in the Basin down the other side of the Divide. You'll be up against it to get range for your horses here."

"I ain't lookin' for range," confessed Ben.

"You're trailin' 'em to market?" The Kid inquired.

"Yes," said Ben. "I—I stole 'em!"

He met The Kid's look squarely.

The wind, freshening, as the night deepened, moaned in the forest and sent sparks from the fire in whirling clouds over their heads. Suddenly from near at hand came the sound of horses. Marcy leaped to his feet with a wild look, his hand dropping to the butt of his gun, and fear shining in his eyes. The Kid rose and looked at him sharply. For a moment he hesitated. The pound of hoofs rode louder on the wind.

"Get back into the timber!" The Kid commanded. "Hurry up—slope!"

Then, as Marcy raced out of the circle of light and into the black shadow of the trees at the upper edge of the meadow, The Kid went quietly about his task of cleaning his few cooking utensils and tin dishes.

Shortly afterward four riders broke into the clearing, brought their horses to a rearing stop near the fire, and covered The Kid with their guns.

"Shucks, that ain't him!"

The Kid recognized the voice, and looked up to meet the peculiar gaze of the big man who had attempted to belittle him in the resort in Dry Crossing that night.

"How do you know it ain't me?" he drawled, hitching his cartridge belt and looking at the others with a tantalizing smile.

The big man and two others put away their guns. Another man, who pushed his horse forward a bit, rested his weapon on the horn of his saddle and regarded The Kid keenly.

"Where you from?" he demanded sharply.

"I reckon I live here," replied The Kid in his exaggerated drawl.

The other scowled. "I'm the sheriff of Musselshell County," he announced sternly; "an' I'm looking for a man about your size an' age who stole some horses from the Tittinger Ranch."

16

"Does the description fit me, sheriff?" asked The Kid blandly.

"No, it doesn't fit you," said the sheriff angrily; "but you might be travelin' with the man it does fit."

"I travel alone," flashed The Kid with a smile.

"You ain't seen any one ridin' this way?"

"I ain't seen anybody ridin' this way, or any way, 'cept you gents," said The Kid firmly, his gaze narrowing.

The sheriff scowled. Another man, who had dismounted and looked over the camp, spoke up.

"Only been one eatin' here," he said gruffly. "Only been one flopping in that tent. Maybe he ain't got this far."

"He's had time enough," growled the sheriff.

"I saw this Kid in a place down at the Crossing," said the big man to the official. "He was alone. They call him The Spectacular Kid, an' I ain't never heard of him being down south. He's from over east somewheres."

Again The Kid encountered a peculiar look in the big man's eyes. It puzzled him. Had his thoughtless gun-drawing display made the man afraid of him? He sensed from the man's manner that this was not so.

The sheriff was gazing at The Kid with undisguised interest.

"I don't figure a gun fighter would be too good to travel with a hoss thief, at that," he muttered.

The Kid's face went white under its tan. He strode closer to the official, disregarding the other's warning movement with his gun.

"That gun wouldn't do you no good, sheriff, if I

wanted to get you," he said grimly. "But I ain't wantin' to get anybody; an' I ain't out gun fightin'. You an' the rest of 'em have hung that title on me, an' I can't help myself; but I'm tellin' you an' the rest of 'em—*don't make me an outlaw!*"

The sheriff was taken back momentarily by the ring of sincerity in the boy's voice and the flashing fire in his eyes. Then he put up his weapon.

"You can make an outlaw of yourself without any trouble, if that hoss thief comes along an' you help him out," he called to The Kid, as he turned his horse. Then he led the little cavalcade at a brisk pace toward the trail leading to the pass over the Divide.

The hoofbeats died away, and again the only sound was that of the wind in the timber. The Kid stood for several minutes looking up at the sky. His face showed a mixture of emotions—anger, loneliness, indecision, and doubt. Truth was, The Kid longed for the companionship of one of his own age. The dubious reputation bestowed upon him had kept him off the ranches in the Basin. There was no work for him in the forest reserve. He could not bring himself to go far away where he was not known, for he loved these hills. And there was another tie, he reflected—with a softening of his features and a sad look in his eyes—which held him there and lured him frequently to a little cabin in a flower-splashed meadow near the falls of the Tenderfoot.

From the shadow of the timber came a soft whistle. The Kid walked toward the place where the signal had been sounded.

"I heard what they said," whispered Marcy. "I knew you wasn't an out-and-out killer, an' I came up here because I liked you an' wanted company. But I'll go quick, so I can't get you in bad."

"This your first job?" asked The Kid. "If it is, there's a chance for you to get into better business. I'd hate a horse thief."

Marcy sucked in his breath. "I took 'em because Tittinger ain't paid me a cent of wages in a year. He tried to drive me off the ranch when I told him I had to have my pay. I took 'em to get even an' get my money. I was sore. There's only three of 'em."

"You mean to say this Tittinger don't pay his men?"

"There ain't a man workin' for him that's been paid up to this spring," declared Marcy. "I reckon he figures he's got to get me, or the rest of the outfit'll run off a big bunch of stock to get what's comin' to 'em. Anyway, I figure he's almost broke. They've had three bad years down there. If you think I'd better do it, I'll hustle the horses back to him."

"Liable to get you in mighty wrong if you don't," said The Kid.

"Maybe I'll do it," said Marcy. "An' listen! That big fellow that was talkin', an' that you met down in town, was Mort Bloomquin. He's a bad one. I don't know what the game is for him to be traveling with that sheriff, for he's been rustlin' stock for years. An' he's a gunman, too—fastest in the Musselshell country, they say."

The Kid whistled softly. It increased the mystery of Bloomquin's peculiar manner toward him, both in town and when he rode up with the sheriff's posse.

Suddenly they were startled, as a horseman rode into the clearing, and a guttural laugh floated to their ears.

The Kid's right hand darted to the ivory butt of his gun.

"No need to draw," said a heavy voice.

The wind caught up the embers and fanned them into flame. The Kid and Marcy gave vent to exclamations, as they recognized the figure in the saddle. It was Bloomquin!

CHAPTER III
A VEILED INVITATION

Leisurely the big man dismounted, while The Kid regarded him with a puzzled frown, and Marcy stood ill at ease. Then Bloomquin loosened the cinch of his saddle and let the bridle reins hang free, so his mount would not stray.

"Let's perk the fire up a bit, so we can see each other, while we're talkin'," he said.

Without waiting for the two to assent he threw some wood upon the smoldering blaze. As the light from the fire lit up their faces, he looked at Marcy curiously.

"You needn't be scared, young fellow," he said loudly with a twisted grin; "I told 'em I'd hit back along this way an' keep an' eye out for you. But that don't mean that I'm goin' to see you," he added with a wink.

The Kid found himself disliking the man's air of intimacy and the veiled insinuations in his words. He disliked Bloomquin's attempt to make his tones seem reassuring—the subtle hint that there might be something between all three of them. Instinctively he felt that here was a man who would resort to shady ways to carry out his enterprises, and who could not be trusted.

"Where's the sheriff an' his outfit hittin' for?" The Kid asked coldly.

Bloomquin eyed him speculatively. "They're goin' down to Jerome on the other side of the Divide," he said finally. "If they find out Marcy ain't been along that way, they'll come back over the pass an' go on up north a ways before turnin' back. I 'spect they'll hear plenty about you when they hit Jerome, eh?"

The Kid resented Bloomquin's chuckle. "I don't care what they hear," he said stoutly. "I killed 'Spike' Harmon fair in a square gun play. If I hadn't killed him, he'd sure 'ave bored me. He—"

The Kid's words died away, as he noted with astonishment the fierce gleam in Bloomquin's eyes.

"How'd you two get mixed up?" demanded Bloomquin in a hoarse voice.

"He killed my foster father, Fred Renault, in a dirty gun play," replied The Kid grimly. "Then he tried to blame him for the rustlin' that's been goin' on in the foothills over there, an' he tried to jail me for the Jericho mine robbery—something I didn't pull off. But he made his biggest mistake when he tried to beat me to the draw, Bloomquin."

21

"I see our friend has been tellin' you my name," sneered the big man.

"Why not?" asked Marcy.

"Sure," said Bloomquin, once more agreeable. "Do you know who *was* doin' the rustlin'?" he asked The Kid quickly.

"I've got my suspicions," answered The Kid, "but I ain't tellin' 'em."

"That's the idear," said Bloomquin, grinning again.

"Did you come up with that posse lookin' for Ben?" The Kid asked.

Bloomquin scowled. "No," he replied shortly. "I just rode along with 'em from Dry Crossin'. I ain't travelin' with no sheriffs." He gave them a meaning look. Then he turned to Marcy.

"I saw you when you was in that place down there, even if you did keep your back turned after I came in. I don't blame you none for takin' them hosses. I'd done the same thing, if old Tittinger owed me money—only I'd taken a lot more." Here he grinned again and winked at them familiarly.

"Suppose us three now was to see a chance to do ourselves some good," he said suavely. "I ain't up here for my health; they've got the goods on you, Marcy; an' The Kid here is in bad. You might as well get blamed for something you did as to hold the sack for something you didn't do, Kid."

The Kid saw a cunning light in the man's eyes. It aroused his curiosity. Why had he seemed to flame with passion when the killing of Harmon was mentioned? Why was he in that locality? Why did he want to shield Ben Marcy? And what was the nature of the veiled proposition he had voiced?

"I get your words, but I don't seem to catch their meanin'," he said.

"You got to think over 'em," said Bloomquin with a smirk. "You're packin' a fast gun an' a hard reputation; you oughter be able to think."

He lent emphasis to his words with another wink.

"Him," he continued, nodding toward Marcy, "he ain't quite so smart. But he's got nerve, an' that's a mighty good asset sometimes."

"It didn't take much nerve to get away with them hosses, if that's what you mean," Marcy put in. "I figured I had 'em comin' to me, an' I just naturally made away with 'em."

"Sure," nodded Bloomquin; "but you got away with 'em slick. That sheriff wouldn't ever took it you'd head this way, if he hadn't been tipped off by one of them high-tension line riders you didn't see, but who saw you. It wasn't a half bad trick at that, boy."

"Listen here, Bloomquin, where's all this talkin' headin' to?" asked The Kid, frowning.

A look akin to admiration flashed in the big man's eyes.

"You're my kind of folks," he said, walking to his horse. He cinched his saddle. With the reins in his left hand resting on his horse's neck, and the stirrup in his right, he turned toward them.

"Suppose you keep low—or, anyways, suppose Marcy keeps low, an' when the sheriff an' his men come back over the Divide you sneak down to

Jerome. I'll see you over there an' everything will be all right."

With this mysterious advice he mounted and spurred his horse across the clearing to the trail which led over the pass, down to the little town of Jerome on the eastern slope, and with the Jericho mine above it.

"I'd like to know what he's gettin' at," said The Kid; "an', what's more, I'm goin' to find out."

"He's got a hard reputation down in the Mussel-shell," declared Ben, who also was puzzled. "He acted funny when you told him about shootin' that man, Harmon."

The Kid was thinking hard. "I don't reckon you better sleep in the tent," he reflected. "I think Bloomquin was tellin' the truth when he said we needn't be scared of him; but Renault taught me to play safe."

"Who was Renault?" Marcy asked curiously.

The Kid hesitated. Although naturally cautious, he reflected that here was a youth in trouble like himself, and he yearned to confide in some one. He told Marcy about Renault, the gambler, who had brought him up after his father had died, when he was ten years old.

"It was Renault who taught me how to draw and shoot an' ride a horse; but he never taught me any bad tricks," said The Kid, while Marcy listened in wonder.

Then The Kid explained how Renault had been killed in an unfair gun play by Spike Harmon; how Harmon had tried to fasten upon Renault the blame for rustling operations east of the Divide; how he had tried to get him, The Kid, taken to jail for the robbery of the

Jericho mine paymaster, and, last, how he, The Kid, had forced the fact that Harmon had killed his foster father out of "Pinky" Swift, a crooked gambler in Jerome, and had later killed Harmon, not so much for revenge as to protect his own life.

However, The Kid failed to mention the Reynolds cabin in the flower-splashed meadow near the falls of the Tenderfoot, and a girl who lived there—a girl whose eyes lighted with a wondrous glow when she saw him riding into the meadow, as he often did. The Reynolds place was a rendezvous inviolate—almost a sanctuary.

"An' now they still think I held up the paymaster an' got away with that money," mused The Kid. He didn't mention that a square gambler, named Parker, had held up the paymaster and then had given back the money in an attempt to divert suspicion from The Kid. Nor did he explain that he had given Parker most of the money left by Renault, so he could send his daughter back East to school.

"An' because I could draw faster'n Harmon, when I had to, or stop lead, they've got me branded as a gun fighter," The Kid concluded bitterly.

Marcy threw an arm about his shoulder, and for a time the two of them were silent. The night wind sang in the timber-clothed slopes, and the last flickering flames of the fire slowly died.

"You better take a couple of those blankets an' sleep out in the timber till daybreak," said The Kid suddenly, leading the way to the tent. "It ain't cold, but you don't want to lay on the ground, I reckon. I've got a pine bed built with a tarp over it, an' that'll fix me up. If they should come back this way they won't find you. There's a little clearin' just below this a ways, where your horse can feed. Where's the other horses?"

Marcy told him they were in a cañon two miles above Dry Crossing, where he had found an old corral and had repaired it.

"I know the place," nodded The Kid. "Now in the morning the sheriff an' his men will be hittin' back over the pass to go north, for they won't find a trace of you in Jerome. Somehow I don't think Bloomquin was lyin'. We'll sneak down an' get those horses an' cache 'em in a place I know up here, where a sheriff couldn't find 'em in a hundred years. By the time he gives up the chase an' goes back, we'll be in Jerome, swingin' our ropes to snare Bloomquin's big idea. You can take the horses back when things calm down a bit. I've got a hunch I know what Bloomquin's up to," concluded The Kid. "An' if my hunch is the goods, I'm powerful concerned."

The Kid gave Marcy the blankets, against his protest, and told him to take his horse from the timber into a little clearing below the meadow and spend the night there.

"It's safer," he said. "I don't expect anybody along, but if some one should happen in before mornin', it's best they don't see you. But I don't reckon that Musselshell hombre will be startin' back this way before an hour or so after sunup, an' they'll be four or five hours on the trail before they get over here."

But The Kid wasn't well enough informed to know

that the Musselshell official wanted Marcy badly, and that the first gray light of dawn would see him and his men on the back trail.

CHAPTER IV
THE SURPRISE

The two youths were stirring before daybreak, Marcy looking after the horses, and The Kid cooking breakfast. Neither intended to sacrifice his appetite to the prospect that the sheriff and his men might show up before they were expected.

The enticing odor of frying bacon and boiling coffee mingled with the faint scent of pine and balsam in the cool, early morning air. Both of the youths plainly relished their surroundings. To Marcy the green of the timber and the stimulating atmosphere of the mountains was something of a novelty, for he had lived mostly in the prairie country. But to The Kid the hills meant home. He had come to the Tenderfoot country with his foster father, Renault, from the flatlands of the Basin to eastward, and they had built a cabin near Jerome, on the eastern slope. But he had lived in the foothills before they had gone to the Basin, and he had known the mystery and lure of the snow-capped peaks and whispering forests all his life.

The sky above the Divide was rosy with the first glow of the dawn, when they finished eating and packed the cooking utensils and the balance of The Kid's belongings. Then they struck the small tent, packed the blankets and other things in it, and cached it in a small, dry cave in the rocks at the foot of the slope behind the camp.

"I had a pack horse along," The Kid explained, "but he got away an' ambled back to—"

He checked his speech. He had come near mentioning the Reynolds rendezvous near Tenderfoot Falls.

"Let's get goin'," he said quickly, and they went for the horses which Marcy had saddled and left in the little clearing below the meadow, where he had spent the night.

The Kid rode ahead down the trail toward the foothills. When he reached a point some distance above the road leading to Dry Crossing, he turned into a dim path leading across a ravine to a fair trail along an opposite ridge. He kept unerringly to the trail, as they came upon other dim paths, and finally Marcy was led to speak in admiration.

"You sure know these mountains," he said. "I came up the road in plain sight when I left the horses down there. An' I was lookin' for a trail, too, but couldn't see any."

"I've been roamin' aroun' here a long time," replied The Kid. "I don't reckon there's anybody hereabouts that knows these hills like I do. We'll cross under the high-tension line, just below here, an' the box cañon, where you cached the horses, is 'bout half a mile below that."

This proved correct, and they found the three horses in the makeshift corral, where Ben had left them. As they drove them down to water, The Kid looked them over critically.

"You sure picked out good stock," he observed.

Marcy grinned. "I was figurin' on gettin' four hundred out of 'em," he confessed. "That's what Tittinger owes me," he added with a frown.

"They're worth all of that," smiled The Kid. "Don't worry about your money. That'll come out all right."

After the horses had been watered The Kid disclosed his plan.

"We'll drive 'em across the cañon under the wires and hit north on a trail that runs under the cliffs below the Divide. I know a blind draw up there where we can cache 'em, so they can't get out. There's water an' feed in there, too. They'll be safe till you want 'em to take 'em back."

They started across the cañon under the wires. Timber and underbrush had been cleared away, leaving a wide swath for the towers and wires of the power line which cut up the slope toward the pass. They passed the worn trail which led to The Kid's camping ground and the pass and continued on to the rock-bound base of the major slope leading to the Divide. Here the timber thinned, and there appeared long stretches of almost level trail in the lee of the rocks. They turned northward toward a point above The Kid's camp site, south of the trail over the pass.

The sun had been shining over the high range above them for some time. The forest was alive with the sound of the wind in the trees and the sharp trill of squirrels sounding their warning. Big blue grouse flew up ahead of them, with a whir of flashing wings, and magpies chattered the news of their passing. The three horses were easily driven on the rock floor of the wide trail. As they proceeded, The Kid kept a sharp lookout and more than once glanced behind them and far ahead along the trail. The hoofs of the three loose horses and his mount and Ben's were making considerable noise. But he reflected that they were some distance from the trail over the pass, and he did not expect the sheriff and his men along for two hours or more.

Ben plainly was nervous, and The Kid wondered at this; for his companion had not hesitated to steal the horses and had driven them many miles. In fact he had shown nerve in practically doubling on his tracks and then swinging into the power trail in bold defiance of his pursuers.

The Kid liked the sandy-haired youth from the lowlands. Ben's clear blue eyes were good eyes, and though they now showed concern—which The Kid believed was mostly felt for him—he had caught the sparkle of love of adventure in them, and he had seen Ben more than once look out over the timbered ranges, with the gaze of a dreamer and a smile of appreciation upon his lips of the wondrous scene.

As they rounded a turn in the trail, The Kid suddenly called out to his companion. Then he whirled his horse and dashed back around the bend, as the faint echoes of shouts came to them from the trail over the pass above them to the north.

"I didn't expect 'em so early," gasped The Kid, as he brought his horse to a stop beside Marcy's. "They saw me. They're coming down the trail from the pass. Now listen, an' I'll tell you what I want you to do."

He paused; and in the interval of silence they again caught the echoes of shouts. The sheriff and his men would ride like mad to the spot, and there was no time to be lost.

"Go back a ways and cut down into the timber," The Kid instructed. "When you get to the timber, edge along north until you hit the trail for the pass. Follow that trail as fast as you can ride. The sheriff an' the others'll cut off the trail an' come along the rocks toward where they saw me—although it was too far for 'em to tell whether it was me or you. While they're off the trail to the pass, tryin' to catch me, you can get up there an' hide in the timber near the pass. I'll be along in a little bit. Now hit for it."

He swung his horse to ride back.

"Wait!" cried Marcy. "Where you goin'?"

"I'm goin' to put the horses in the blind cañon," said The Kid. "Then I'll ride to the trail by a way I know near the top of the Divide an' meet you at the pass."

"You can't do that!" cried Marcy excitedly. "They might catch you, an' then they'd think you was in with me on the hosses. I'll take the hosses myself—or we can drive 'em back—or—"

"No," said The Kid firmly. "They haven't seen you with the horses, an' they've got to catch you with 'em to have the goods on you. I can hide 'em under their noses. Do as I say, Ben," he pleaded; "I know what I'm about. I'll meet you on the trail up near the pass, an' we'll leave 'em down here lookin' for us. They'd never

31

figure we'd hit over the Divide. We ain't got much time to be talkin'. Will you let me handle this deal?"

Marcy hesitated. The shouts were plainer now, and the sound of galloping hoofs rumbled dully on the breeze.

"It'd look bad for 'em to see two of us with the horses," The Kid pointed out. "Then they'd know for sure I was mixed up in it. I can get the horses into the blind cañon without them seein' me, an' then they can look for a week, an' they won't find a trace of us nor the stock. I wouldn't have a pardner that wouldn't listen to reason," he added soberly.

Marcy gulped. His eyes shone. "All right," he decided; "but if I see you from up there gettin' into trouble, I'll come chargin' down to set in on the play."

He rode swiftly for the timber, while The Kid spurred his mount after the horses around the bend. He caught a single glimpse of the riders dashing down the steep trail from the pass. They would swing off the trail, he knew, when they came to the level shelflike space in the lee of the rocky base of the slope. Then they would gallop southward, while he would be hastening the horses in their direction. The hidden opening to the blind draw, where he intended to hide the horses, was about halfway between the bend, where he had separated from Ben Marcy, and the trail to the pass.

Marcy would have ample opportunity to ride around behind the posse and gain the trail near the pass. Meanwhile The Kid would have to beat the sheriff and his men to the opening of the cañon and get in the narrow defile without being seen. Then they could hunt for him!

A smile played upon the youth's lips, and a reckless light of daring was in his eyes. All of his life that he could remember had been like this. From the time of his mother's death, when he was a mere child, he had roamed the cattle camps with his father. And after the death of his father, when Renault had taken charge of him, he had kept to the wild trails of the round-ups, with a few months every year or two at school in some cow town.

Then they had come to the hills, and The Kid had roamed the wild fastnesses of the mountains, spent days in the cabin near Jerome, reading, while the snows of the fierce Northern winter piled upon the ridges; and he had worked on the range, while Renault made excursions to the cities of the Basin to gamble. He had had little companionship save that of Renault and the girl, Lettie Reynolds, near the falls of Tenderfoot Creek.

Now had come Ben Marcy, and The Kid had liked him from the start. Ben was in trouble. Something within the boy's heart seemed to swell. This was the manner in which lasting friendships were made in the West, was it not? And Marcy had come when The Kid was lonely—uncertain what to do. And Bloomquin! The Kid's face drew into grim lines. A cattle thief! Could Bloomquin help him prove that Renault had not been a rustler?

These thoughts flashed through The Kid's mind, as he drove the horses at the fastest possible pace, doing some masterful riding on the big gray, "Ironsides." He was heading them straight for the opening of the blind cañon.

Now he could not see the posse, for it had gained the rock shelf and was galloping toward him, screened by intervening bends and clumps of timber. But now and again he could hear the sounds of plunging horses in that wild ride to head him off. But did they now know that he was riding toward them?

It was a race to gain the entrance to the cañon. Once inside, The Kid believed he would be safe. The posse would dash past his hiding place—would assume he had turned back or had sought refuge in the timbered slopes below. They would scatter and search, and he would calmly ride to join Marcy.

Sounds of the oncoming riders became more and more distinct. The Kid drove the horses, as he had never driven stock before. They were wild with fear and excitement, putting their utmost into their efforts; but they could not run as fast as the big gray could have pushed them.

The Kid rounded a clump of boulders and dashed for the screen of firs before the opening to the cañon. The horses plunged through, but as The Kid followed, the sharp barking of six-shooters sounded above the pound of hoofs, and a rain of bullets whined about him, clipping twigs and branches which fell in a shower. As the green screen closed about him, The Kid heard the booming voice of the sheriff:

"Trapped! By gad, we've got him!"

He rode on through the defile with bullets whistling overhead.

CHAPTER V
THE SHALE

In the flashing glimpse The Kid had obtained of the posse, as he dashed into the timber screen, The Kid had seen three riders. These must be the sheriff and his two men, he decided. Bloomquin, then, was not with them. So far Bloomquin had spoken the truth; for he had said the sheriff was going to Jerome, and that he, Bloomquin, was traveling with the posse temporarily and would remain at Jerome.

The Kid now was in a narrow defile on a smooth trail, except for bushes and buckbrush and occasional boulders. This entrance to the blind draw above was cleverly concealed in what appeared to be a solid wall of rock from below; but now that the posse had seen him enter, it was no longer to be viewed as a hiding place. If he could have got in without being seen, everything would have been all right. But his secret had been discovered.

The firing behind ceased. The sheriff evidently figured that he had him trapped. But The Kid could hear the sound of the horses ridden by his pursuers. They were not far in the rear. This fact brought The Kid to swift realization of his danger. He was now in possession of the stolen horses. If captured with them he would be accused of complicity with Marcy in their theft. That would mean prison; and to one of The Kid's wild spirit that would be as bad as death.

He did not believe, however, that his pursuers had secured a good enough view of him to be certain that it was he, and not Marcy, who was driving the horses. The thing to do was to get away, but how?

The trail became strewn with rocks and boulders, gradually increasing in size until they nearly choked the narrow defile between the towering walls on either side. It was impossible to proceed faster than at a walk. The three horses ahead did not have to be driven now, or headed off and kept in point; they had but one way to go—ahead.

As they wound around the boulders and squeezed through gaps, scarcely wider than a horse, The Kid racked his brains for a plan which would enable him to shake off the posse. In the end he was compelled to concede to himself that this would be impossible in the blind draw. He knew the head of the draw too well. It was an almost perpendicular slope of fine, sliding shale rock. Its sides were masses of boulders except in one place on the right, where a horse could get halfway up the side of the shale slope. But to drive the horses up there and try to drive them across the shale would mean that they would end in a sliding, tumbling, rolling mass on the rocks at the foot of the slope. To attempt this was out of the question; for to kill the horses would make the offense of stealing them almost secondary, and place further responsibility upon Ben Marcy, which The Kid had no wish to do.

Immersed in these thoughts which concerned the stolen horses, The Kid suddenly cried aloud with dismay. He had forgotten about getting out himself!

And he had passed the trail which branched off from the defile and wound up the steep sides to the left and out to the flank of the main ridge of the Divide. His own escape was shut off.

With the chilling realization of his dangerous predicament, The Kid's lips froze into a white line. He spurred the big gray ahead at every opportunity offered. He came to two huge boulders and squeezed through. Then, dismounting, he crept to a vantage point among the rocks above the trail. In less than a minute the form of the sheriff showed in the trail below, and then two other riders, whom The Kid recognized as the sheriff's deputies, came into view.

A bullet from The Kid's gun clipped a splinter from the face of a boulder a foot ahead of the sheriff's horse. Two more bullets whistled past the sheriff and his men, and they broke for cover behind the rocks. The Kid finished with two more shots in their direction and leaped nimbly back down to his horse.

"That'll slow 'em up," he muttered, as he swung into the saddle.

He rode on, reloading his gun. But he knew the pursuit was halted only temporarily. The posse would soon learn he had fled his point of vantage, and they would push on. He gazed up at the sheer walls of rock above the boulders on either side of the narrow defile. His escape was effectively cut off so far as getting up those walls was concerned. He didn't waste time considering it. His heart beat hopefully, as he realized that he could check the pursuit of the posse at any time within the defile by subjecting the riders to his fire. But such a check would merely result in their starving him out, or sending for reinforcements. No, he had to make a clean getaway.

Realizing now that he was a good two minutes ahead of the sheriff and his deputies, a daring plan suggested itself to The Kid. He pushed forward up the trail, where the defile widened out into the draw, or pocket cañon. He could see this point somewhat above, its location marked by a stunted pine which leaned from a towering rock out-cropping. He spurred the big gray, and the horse raced up the last remaining bit of steep trail and came out into the draw.

The three horses were there, trotting about in a circle, wild and frightened. The Kid's eye roved over the enclosed confines of the draw. The shale slope shone dull and gray under the rib of rock which buttressed the high, bare ridge of the Divide. It was a veritable pocket hewn out of the mountain. Northward, beyond the pass, the summit of Milestone Peak looked coldly down upon the flowing ridges supporting it.

For a moment The Kid hesitated, then he rode swiftly to a point above the three horses. Drawing his gun he began to shout. Then he drove in his steel and dashed down upon the startled horses, firing several shots. The horses whirled and made for the trail out of the draw. The Kid kept at their heels, shouting and firing. The maddened animals plunged down the trail, too frightened to be careful of the twists and turns among the boulders—sliding, slipping, leaping and careening in the narrow path. From below, The Kid heard shouts, and he pressed close behind the horses, reloading his gun. Would the maddened beasts overrun the posse?

Suddenly a new factor entered into his bold play. A gun was barking from the top of the rock wall on the north side of the defile! He came to the two huge boulders and clambered to his former vantage point, where he had checked the posse with his gun. He saw the horses plunging down the trail, saw the three members of the posse, riding before them, dart to safety among the boulders, where they had sought protection from his bullets. The horses swept on down the trail and disappeared to the rumble of madly flying hoofs.

More shots came from the ridge above, and lead spattered on the rocks where the sheriff and his men had taken refuge. They began to return the fire. The Kid surmised at once that Marcy had ridden along the ridge from the pass and was risking his life to help him. Would the sheriff assume that it was he, The Kid, who was on the ridge? Or would he take after the horses?

These questions were quickly answered when, in a lull in the firing, the sheriff himself dashed out from behind the boulders and made for the next favorable shelter up the trail. Several bullets rained about him, as he turned his horse behind a shaft of rock below the two huge boulders.

The Kid didn't wait for further evidence that the sheriff intended to continue up the trail. He slipped down and mounted the big gray, and turned him up the trail. In a few minutes he gained the little draw. He paused, patting the neck of his horse, gazing with narrowed eyes at the treacherous slope of shale at the head of the draw.

To go back would mean that he would have to stop the posse with bullets. He did not wish to kill. He shuddered at the thought. But he would have to wound or kill, if he was to pass back that way. His ruse to force his pursuers back by driving the horses upon them— force them back past the point where the trail led up the cliffs out of the defile—had failed, because of that one wide space in the trail. And the sheriff knew he could not gain the top of that rock wall in such an amazingly short space of time. The sheriff knew he was still somewhere up the trail.

The Kid's face was pale under its heavy coating of tan.

To go back would mean capture, unless he wounded or killed all three men in the posse. And Marcy, seeing him in the dash for freedom, would certainly try to make his bullets count in his favor. Both their hands would be stained with crimson and the stigma of outlawism stamped upon them.

Grimly he faced about. Then he urged the gray up the steep trail to the right of the shale slope. Higher and higher he mounted, with the echoes of shots and shouts coming to his ears from below. The posse was nearing the draw. He paused at the highest point in the treacherous trail and scanned the face of the shale slope. It was perhaps fifteen yards wide at this point. On the other side the ridge had flattened off, offering firm footing for several yards up and down the slope, and it slanted gradually to the top. Once across it, The Kid could ride to safety.

The thunder of hoofs on the rocky trail below came

to his ears. A minute more and the posse would be in the draw. The Kid lifted his feet from the stirrups, turned the magnificent gray toward the slope, and drove in his spurs.

The gray leaped upon the shale, slid, and leaped again. There was a loud pur of masses of fine rock rattling downward. A fine dust rose in a cloud enveloping horse and rider. The gray slipped upon his side, as The Kid lifted his right leg free. Then the big animal gathered its strength and ploughed, sliding and slipping, up to its knees in the shale.

As he felt the play of mighty muscles beneath him, The Kid held his breath. He cried out encouragement to his mount. The dust cloud thickened, and the noise of the loosened rock became a roar. He could not see the draw below, but he heard a wild chorus of shouts and yells. There were shots and bullets flying past him. Then more shots from higher up. Marcy had moved up the ridge and again was supporting him and diverting attention with his fire. The shouts receded, and The Kid knew the posse had ducked to cover under the ledge below the stunted pine.

The big gray was more than halfway across. The Kid felt a thrill, as he realized the shale had a firm base. But they were slipping down the slope! If they slipped past the point on the other side, where the ridge flattened out, they would slide to death among the rocks below.

"Ironsides!" he shouted, with a sob in his voice.

The big gray responded with every iota of his powerful strength. His leap sent a shower of shale from his hoofs, and the boy could hear the fine rock thundering

41

down with a dull roar of an avalanche. The dust was stifling; he could see nothing save his horse's head and neck, dimly outlined through the pall which was stained a sickly saffron by the rays of the sun.

Then the horse struck a firmer footing and again plunged ahead. More shale! The fifteen yards of treacherous rock particles seemed miles in length to the desperate youth. One way or the other he wanted the ordeal over. And in that moment, when death hovered in the shadow of the dust, he thought of the cool, flower-splashed meadow where a cabin nestled.

Now came the gritting of shod hoofs on solid rock. The big gray straightened, shook himself, trotted up the ridge above the dust cloud. Something in the boy's throat tightened, and his heart gave a great bound, as his mount topped the ridge and stopped near a clump of wind-blown pines out of sight of the men in the draw below.

The Kid was still sitting quietly in his saddle, when Ben Marcy came running up to him.

CHAPTER VI
NEAR THE PASS

I was goin' to start shootin' in earnest when they began poppin' at you, as you were crossin' that shale," grinned Marcy. "I reckon they knew it by the way they hit for cover. I didn't have any idea you could make it. You've got some hoss," he added, looking the big gray over in open admiration.

The Kid dismounted and rubbed Ironsides on his nose. The big horse was quivering after his tremendous exertions in the sliding rock of the slope.

"Take a look down there an' see if you can spot the posse," said The Kid to Ben. "I don't think they knew if it was me or you with the horses, for the dust was pretty bad when I came across. But they're pretty dumb, if they don't know we're sort of travelin' together by now. What with me leadin' 'em a wild chase down there, an' you tryin' to pot-shot 'em from up here, I reckon they've got suspicious, even if they don't know which is which."

Marcy laughed. "I didn't figure on lettin' you get caught with the hosses, if I could help it," he said, sobering. "But this shootin' to hit folks is bad business."

The Kid nodded. "I've never gone for my gun yet till the other man started for his," he mused. "An' they're callin' me a gun fighter."

Marcy looked at him queerly for a moment, then he hurried up the ridge and peered down into the draw far below. He could see no one.

"Can't spot 'em," he told The Kid cheerfully when he returned. "Maybe they figure on comin' aroun' up here after us."

The Kid mounted and waited, while Marcy got his own horse which he had left in the timber, while he crawled to the top of the ridge.

"I came over when I heard some shots," he explained to The Kid. "I was waitin' for you near the pass."

The Kid led the way through the scant timber growth

43

above the draw to a dim game trail which ran along just under the crest of the Divide. They followed this until they gained a point a short distance south of the pass and nearly above it. Here they waited, keeping a sharp lookout below. Before the morning was much further advanced, The Kid pointed out a figure riding up the trail toward the pass.

"Looks like the sheriff from here," he observed. "Maybe he's goin' over to Jerome to get some more men to help hunt for us."

Shortly afterward, while the man in the saddle continued up the trail, Marcy detected the other two members of the posse in a large meadow below the rock trail at the entrance to the blind cañon. These men appeared to be herding the stolen horses.

"They've got the horses anyway," he said. "That'll save me the trouble of takin' 'em back."

"I thought it would be a good plan to let 'em have 'em," said The Kid. "Now they've got the stock, maybe they won't be so particular 'bout gettin' you. Tittinger is four hundred to the good, you see."

Marcy shook his head doubtfully. "The sheriff wants to make a showin'," he said. "There's been a lot of queer deals pulled down in the Musselshell without nobody gettin' in jail, an' I reckon he just naturally thinks I'd make a good example."

The Kid rose and beckoned to his companion. He pushed his way afoot up a precarious trail to the crest of the Divide. They were thousands of feet high here and on a level with the shoulders of Milestone Peak on the other side of the pass. They could see the ridges falling away to eastward, with the far-flung prairies of the Basin beyond.

The Kid pointed out the approximate location of the town of Jerome and his cabin a few miles northeast of the village. They could look almost directly down into the pass and could see a great deal of the trail leading down to Jerome. There was another trail—a trail over the north shoulder of Milestone, some miles to northward—which The Kid did not mention. This was a secret trail known, so far as he was aware, only to himself. It led over the Divide to the cabin on Tenderfoot Creek.

Marcy exclaimed suddenly, while The Kid was gazing toward the great peak and the country beyond:

"Somebody's ridin' up the trail from Jerome!" he cried excitedly.

The Kid looked and saw a horseman coming up the trail. Looking on the other side he found he was able to identify the first rider as the Musselshell sheriff. The rider approaching from the east looked like Bloomquin, and in a few minutes both youths recognized the burly figure in the saddle as the gunman from the south.

"Whatever's up, we've got a grandstand seat," said The Kid. "The man you're afraid of is coming from the west, an' the man I want to get a line on is comin' from the east. They'll just about meet on the east side of the pass, where we can see 'em good. Too bad we ain't down where we could hear what they'll have to say to each other."

He gazed down the sheer rock wall into the pass,

realizing with a frown that it would be utter folly to attempt to get within earshot of the two riders who would meet below. They waited expectantly, and, as The Kid had predicted, Bloomquin and the sheriff met on the east side of the pass. They stopped, and the pair watching from above could see they were engaged in an argument. Bloomquin appeared the more aggressive of the two. He made many emphatic gestures and occasionally swung an arm toward the western end of the pass.

"Whatever Bloomquin's got up his sleeve, I don't know," The Kid whispered to Marcy; "but he's tryin' to steer the sheriff away from the east side."

"An' he's doin' it!" said Ben hoarsely. "Look—the sheriff is turning back!"

The official had swung his horse about and seemed on the point of starting back through the pass.

"Listen!" exclaimed The Kid. "I'm goin' to slip down an' follow Bloomquin. You stay here an' keep your eyes out till I signal you to come down. I'll wave my hat," he called back, as he started down to where the horses had been left.

He led the big gray slowly down a game trail until he was just above the western end of the pass—on a level almost with the wires of the high-tension power line. He had not seen the sheriff leave the pass, so he waited, screened by some firs and cedar bushes which grew close to the big dent in the ridge. In a few minutes the sheriff passed on the trail below, riding at a fast pace. The Kid waited till he had disappeared from sight down the trail and then quickly led his horse down the remaining distance. He mounted and galloped east-ward through the pass.

As he came out on the other side, he saw Bloomquin in a turn of the trail, a mile or so below him. He gave the big gray the spurs and dashed in pursuit. Although Bloomquin had a good mount and was riding fast, the big gray gained steadily. The Kid wanted to overtake him before he could reach the town of Jerome.

It was in Jerome that The Kid was best known. There he had received his name of gun fighter, and there it still was believed that he had held up the Jericho mines paymaster. He had no desire to enter the town in such a spectacular fashion, for he was not sure of Bloomquin, and he didn't know what charge Ed Mately, the deputy at Jerome, might have ready to put against him.

The big gray covered the trail with the speed of the wind, again arousing the boy's admiration. In less than three miles he came upon Bloomquin, who had stopped and turned his horse and was waiting, his hand on his gun.

Again The Kid saw that mysterious look in the big man's eyes. It baffled him to deduce whether it was anger or cunning, or a combination of both.

"What's the play, Bloomquin?" The Kid asked coldly, coming to the point boldly and without parley. "I saw you talkin' to the sheriff."

"An' you an' that kid from down below nearly messed things up," said Bloomquin, with a frown. "I had a hunch you'd try to move those horses this mornin', an' I rode over to be on hand."

"Meanin' you was goin' to square things off if anything happened?" asked The Kid skeptically.

"I couldn't have squared anything off, if that sheriff had got hold of Marcy," said Bloomquin crisply. "He's in bad. An' you ain't sittin' none too pretty. If you youngsters want to listen to a little reason, maybe I can put something your way."

The Kid nodded. "We suspected you had something up your sleeve; but you're mighty slow lettin' it out."

Bloomquin ignored this remark. "The sheriff is goin' back with the horses," he said with a scowl. "An' I'm goin' back to Jerome. You an' Marcy can use your own judgment."

"That sounds halfway like a threat, Bloomquin," observed The Kid. He studied the glowering visage of the big man, while he built a brown-paper cigarette. Twice Bloomquin seemed on the point of making an angry retort, but he succeeded in holding himself in check.

"Nevertheless, it goes as I said it," he declared finally.

"More reason why we should look at it from all angles," said The Kid coolly. "It ain't often, I take it, that sheriffs are turned aroun' in their tracks as easy as you did the trick."

"If you mean that I'm in with that posse, you're a fool!" cried Bloomquin. "I could have had you both last night if I'd wanted you. I guess you ain't got the head to back up your gun after all." A sneer played upon the big man's thick lips.

"Just the same I ain't takin' your word for anything till I find out more about you," said The Kid stoutly, his right hand resting easily on his thigh near his gun. "A mighty wise hombre taught me to play safe."

In his last two words The Kid had sounded the slogan of his foster father, Fred Renault, which he had adopted for his own.

Bloomquin gazed at him searchingly. "You've got a chance to find more out," he said with a forced smile resembling a smirk. "I'm goin' down to Jerome." He whirled his horse and galloped down the trail.

The Kid sat his mount for a time in silent perplexity. He did not believe that Bloomquin was associated with the sheriff in the hunt for Ben Marcy; but he felt that the big man had some nature of influence with the Musselshell official. Moreover he had a definite purpose in being in that locality. What would it gain him to set a trap for him, The Kid, and Ben Marcy?

As he rode slowly back up the trail to the pass, The Kid pondered the problem. He could arrive at no logical solution. It was evident, however, that any proposition which Bloomquin might have to make to them would not be made for any reason of friendliness or sympathy. The Kid was convinced that Bloomquin inwardly hated him, even though he tried to conceal this on the surface.

It was afternoon when The Kid neared the pass and took off his hat to signal to Marcy. Then he rode into the screen of timber and waited for some time until Marcy appeared.

"They've gone on with the horses," said Marcy, smiling. "Looks like they'd given us up."

In a few words The Kid explained his conversation with Bloomquin. "It's gettin' along in the afternoon, an' we'll hit for my cabin," he concluded. "I wouldn't worry any more about that sheriff unless he shows up again. He's got the horses, an' Bloomquin has given him his papers some way—I can't figure it all out. An' I'm gettin' hungry!"

They turned off the main trail and followed one of the numerous cattle paths through the timber, walking their horses and enjoying the cool air among the trees, scented with balsam and fir. The sun was dipping behind the western ridges when they reached the little clearing wherein was The Kid's cabin. They turned the horses out to graze in the fragrant meadow, with its little stream of clear water, and set about preparing an ample meal from the contents of their slicker packs and the provisions in the cabin. After supper The Kid saddled his horse.

"You stick aroun' here till I get back," he told Ben. "I wouldn't be too generous with lamplight, I reckon. An' I'll sure be back before mornin'."

Then he mounted and rode through the twilight toward Jerome.

CHAPTER VII
A NEW MOVE

Plank's place in Jerome was the most notorious resort in the mountain country. It was here that the heaviest gambling and the hardest fighting were done, and it had to be more than an ordinary fight to be staged in Plank's, for mere brawls were not countenanced. It was a center, too, for scheming and plotting, and a rendezvous for doubtful characters as well as miners and cow-punchers from the surrounding territory.

The town was isolated from most of the county in which it was situated, being separated from the county seat by the Tenderfoot Range. For this reason it had a deputy sheriff, although Ed Mately found his work as an officer handicapped by the peculiar situation of the town and his limited territory. Jerome was nearly at the spot where three counties joined, and the nearest large town was forty-five miles to eastward in the Basin.

It was this wild setting which had attracted Fred Renault—The Kid's foster father—and his friend, Burkin, the gambler. It had attracted others, too, such as Pinky Swift, who made his living at crooked cards, and who had the gaming "privilege" in Plank's.

Strangers came and went. Silent, mysterious characters, many of these; men whom Ed Mately scrutinized carefully, but did not molest. And at this particular time, with the summer drawing to a close and the fall elections looming, Mately was strengthening his political fences in his chief's favor, by discreetly overlooking certain things, as is the custom in the hills before a battle at the polls. Moreover the sheriff at the county seat preferred to pay scant attention to Jerome because of its isolation and the very small amount of news which leaked out of the hills concerning activities there.

Therefore, when The Kid rode into town early that night, he found the place swarming with men from the mines and the surrounding ranges. Everything was wide open, with Plank's and the other resorts running full blast. The Kid hesitated, as he led his horse toward the hitching shed behind Plank's. Finally he turned aside from the shed and led his mount into a patch of timber behind the shed, near the trail which led to his cabin. Before entering the resort he peered through a rear window. The place was crowded, and his view was shut off by a group standing about one of the gaming tables in the rear. He turned to the door and stepped quickly from the shadow outside into the glare of the swinging lamps within. A moment later Ed Mately sauntered up to him from the bar.

"Just passin' through, Kid?" he asked casually.

"Reckon I'm lookin' in," answered The Kid coldly. He resented the deputy's tone.

"I thought you'd cut out this stampin' ground after that Jericho business an' the trouble with Harmon," said Mately. "I don't remember anybody askin' for you aroun' here." He looked at the youth sharply.

"Say, if you're figurin' on scarin' me out, Mately, it

just can't be done," flared the boy. "Anyway I wouldn't quit this country till I'd shown up the crowd that was tryin' to brand Renault as a rustler."

"I'd like to be shown that myself, Kid," said the deputy; "but I don't reckon it's in the pictures. There's too many heard Renault say he'd come up from Dry Fork way, an' we got a few head down there that'd been worked over with a runnin' iron into some peculiar brands. I ain't exactly blamin' you or Renault, but I ain't in the know in this business—yet."

"You're right, you ain't!" exclaimed The Kid. "An' you ain't willin' to believe me, either. I don't ask you to, so far as that goes, Mately; all I'm wantin' is a square deal an' I aim to get that."

"This isn't a time for threats," said Mately meaningly. "You're on thin ice, an' your rep's gone to smash aroun' here. I'd pick softer workin' grounds, Kid. That's my advice."

"Which I ain't askin'," returned the youth, with sarcasm in his tone. "Look here, are you warnin' me off this range, Mately?"

Mately's eye was cold, and his manner aggressive. "Any tip I'm handin' you is for your own good," he said evenly. "One more trick'll do for you in this neck o' the woods. It's time you did less swaggerin' aroun' an' started doin' some thinking."

He moved quickly away, and The Kid saw Bloomquin's dark features in the mirror behind the bar. Then, to his astonishment, he saw Pinky Swift smiling amiably at him from a near-by table, where the gambler was dealing stud poker. He could not understand this show of friendliness on Swift's part, for he had compelled Swift to tell him at the point of his gun the part Spike Harmon had played in the shooting of Renault. By all the rules Swift should hate him. The Kid descried still another interested look from among the many faces. This was Burkin, the old card player who had been his friend and Renault's. He thought he caught a subtle look of warning in the man's gaze.

As the youth strode to the bar, he sensed again that significant feeling that many eyes were upon him; that his presence put a tenseness into the atmosphere of the resort. He had many times in the past witnessed this situation, when a known gunman had entered a crowded place. He felt no thrill of pride that his own entrance should gain him such recognition. The thought of the sinister reputation which had been thrust upon him irritated him and caused him to frown. This narrowing of the eyes and lowering of his brows gave him the typical look of a gun fighter, although he did not realize that such was the effect. He noted with further distaste that men made room for him at the bar.

His characteristic demand for "something soft" caused no surprise here. The bartender served him without question, setting out the cold lemon soda, with the same respect with which he would have put out the bottle of forbidden white liquor. Nor were there any audible comments on The Kid's preferred refreshment.

Meanwhile the youth continually sought Bloomquin's eyes in the mirror. The big man was standing at the upper end of the bar near the front entrance to the place. While he looked significantly at The Kid he made no move to engage him in conversation, or to give any one the impression that they had ever met before. All of which was puzzling and annoying to the youth who had come to Jerome to compel Bloomquin to show his hand.

Burkin had relinquished his place at one of the tables and was standing near the rear door. The Kid saw Pinky Swift and Mately, who had not gone out, regarding him covertly. The whole situation now suddenly amused him. His face broke into a smile. Then it was he caught Bloomquin staring darkly at him, and a moment later the big man turned from the bar and went out of the front door.

The Kid caught a significant flash from Burkin's eyes, and a moment later he strolled past the old gambler and went out the rear way. Soon afterward Burkin slipped quietly out into the shadows. The older man grasped The Kid warmly by the hand.

"What's brought you back here, Kid?" he asked anxiously. "I'm mighty glad to see you, but you're takin' a chance in comin' here where Pinky and his crowd have it in for you."

"What's Pinky been up to lately?" asked the boy, peering about in the shadows to make sure they were not observed.

"I don't know," Burkin confessed. "I don't pay much attention to him an' any of his gang. This town is a sort of a last resort for me, an' I don't aim to put myself in bad if I can help it. But, listen, Kid, you're in danger here!"

The old gambler whispered the words of warning in

a hoarse voice and looked furtively about. They were standing in the shadow of the trees near a back window of the resort darkened by a heavy curtain.

"The big fellow that was standing at the upper end of the bar," Burkin went on; "I saw him talkin' with Mately this afternoon. An' tonight I happened to overhear him conversing with Swift at the hotel. He's got it in for you, Kid, for you shootin' Spike Harmon. I heard him tell Swift he'd get you right, then I had to slip away so's they wouldn't see me. He's dangerous, that fellow, Kid—I know his looks."

"I'm trailin' him," The Kid confessed in a worried tone. "I'm tryin' to find out what he's here for."

Then he whispered the details of his meetings with Bloomquin, while the gambler listened eagerly.

"I'm goin' to force his hand," he concluded. "I'm much obliged to you for your tip, an' I wish you'd keep your eyes open, Mr. Burkin. If Bloomquin had wanted to get me fair an' square, he had his chance. He's got something up his sleeve, an' Ben an' I are goin' to find out what it is."

"He wants you to go into some kind of a deal with him?" Burkin said softly, half to himself. "I'd be careful, Kid. He ain't playin' in the open, an' this ain't a good time for you to be gettin' mixed up in anything off color. Mately's layin' for you. He knows he could make trouble for you without gettin' in bad with the powers aroun' here, an' he has to make a showin' at the county seat. You got to watch your step pretty close. I don't like the looks of Pinky Swift giving you the glad welcome, like he did tonight. I was watching him."

A faint stir among the trees near at hand made them both alert. They drew farther back into the shadows of the cottonwoods near the rear of the building, Burkin pressing The Kid's arm to caution him. In a few moments a figure slipped from the trees near the horse shed. It stole quietly to the rear window, from which came a gleam of yellow light. This was the window on the farther side of the door, some distance from the darkened window where The Kid and Burkin had stood, secreted in the dense shadow. A shaft of the yellow light shone full on the face of the newcomer and caused both The Kid and Burkin to start.

After a long look inside, the man stepped quickly away from the window and walked stealthily around the corner of the building toward the short main street of the little town.

"Curt Donald, deputy sheriff from the county seat!" The Kid exploded in a guarded voice.

"That beats me," murmured Burkin nervously. "I can't understand why he's here."

"I'm goin' around for a look," said The Kid.

There was a sharp cracking of underbrush. As The Kid whirled with his hand on his gun, there came a sharp command.

"Put 'em up!" was the order, as three figures stepped from the deeper shadow.

The Kid hesitated, but obeyed, when he made out the bulky form of Bloomquin.

CHAPTER VIII
ON THE DRY FORK

To The Kid's surprise, Bloomquin himself appeared undeniably astonished when he discovered the identity of the pair he and his men had accosted.

"Thought you was inside," he growled at The Kid, putting up his gun.

The Kid could see the man's face dimly in the half light from the stars. Bloomquin plainly was nettled. He was staring at Burkin, with a deep frown, apparently suspicious and perplexed.

"You were expecting to find some one else here?" asked Burkin quietly. He, too, had surmised that Bloomquin was irritated because of his presence. "I was giving my young friend here some advice about buckin' the games hereabouts."

The Kid laughed softly. His forced mirth had an immediate effect upon Bloomquin.

"If you're done, I'll talk to The Kid myself," he snapped to Burkin.

"Go ahead," said The Kid quickly to his friend. "Bloomquin an' I'll go inside."

"That ain't necessary," Bloomquin blurted, striving to control himself. "But it's all up to you, Kid, whether you want to talk to me or not. I ain't aimin' to make you do anything by force. I was mistaken as to who you two were—that's all. Your friend, here, can believe me or not; I ain't doin' any more explaining."

The Kid noticed that Burkin had slipped his right hand into his right-side coat pocket. He smiled, as he remembered the gambler was accustomed to carrying an old-fashioned, but efficient, derringer in that pocket. But Bloomquin's explanation puzzled him exceedingly. Had the big man really been mistaken in their identity? Had he left the resort and hurried around to the rear to join his men waiting there because he anticipated the arrival of some one else? Curt Donald, perhaps? Or had the presence of Burkin caused Bloomquin hastily to change his plans?

"I reckon you'd better leave me with Bloomquin," he said firmly to Burkin. "Whatever he's got to say, I came down here to hear it."

The old gambler hesitated.

The two men with Bloomquin had retired a little distance. The affair had lost its first appearance of serious aggressiveness.

"There's a back room in Plank's that ain't being used now," he suggested.

"An' there's a hundred men or so in there to watch us goin' into it," snapped Bloomquin. "I'll be moving, Kid, unless you want to come along."

"I'm goin'," said The Kid. "But I don't reckon we've got to have any guards along; do you, Bloomquin?"

The big man caught the significance of the query instantly.

"Beat it!" he said to the pair behind him without looking around.

The two men moved swiftly around the dark corner of the building toward the front. Burkin appeared relieved. He withdrew his hand from his pocket.

"You'll look me up before you go away again?" he asked the boy.

"I sure will," promised The Kid. "An' you might keep an eye on my cabin, if I'm gone long." He knew by the old gambler's pressure on his arm that he understood. He would get word to Ben Marcy, and the two of them would begin to search for him, if he was to be gone for any length of time.

Burkin left them, and Bloomquin led the way to the horse shed.

"Where's that young Marcy?" he asked suddenly.

The Kid started. Had Bloomquin thought it was Ben Marcy standing with him in the shadows of Plank's place?

"I ain't quite sure," he evaded.

Bloomquin swung upon him, and the youth could see the big man's face glowering darkly in the dim light.

"This ain't no time for lying, Kid," said Bloomquin savagely.

The Kid's mind was keenly alert. He was not afraid of Bloomquin alone. Perhaps the big man would welcome the chance to talk to himself and Ben at his cabin.

"Marcy may be up at my place, if you want to take a ride up there with me," he replied.

"Somebody was up there lookin' for you, an' there wasn't nobody home," said Bloomquin in a sneering tone. Evidently he thought The Kid was trying to put him off the track.

"How long since?" asked the boy, genuinely interested. "I left him there."

For a space Bloomquin was silent. Then: "You're sure?" he asked doubtfully.

"Sure and certain sure," answered The Kid convincingly.

"Well, if you left him there, he's beat it," said Bloomquin. "I sent those two men up there before dark looking for you. Guess they didn't get the right trail at first, but they found the cabin after sunset, an' there wasn't nobody there. Wasn't any horses there, either. You sure Marcy didn't ride down with you? I guess you came down by a short cut. They tell me you know every footpath an' cow track aroun' here."

"I left Marcy there," said The Kid in a troubled voice. "He might have struck out into the timber, thinkin' it was safer."

"Well, we don't need him yet," said Bloomquin. He thought for a minute. "Kid, you want to take a little ride with me?" he asked earnestly.

"That depends, Bloomquin. I ain't doin' much ridin' just for pleasure."

"But you'd ride if you thought it might help you to prove that Fred Renault wasn't doin' any rustlin', wouldn't you?" Bloomquin interrupted eagerly.

"I'd ride a long ways to prove that," said The Kid soberly.

"That's why I want you to go with me," said Bloomquin, raising his voice a bit in his eagerness. "Maybe I can help you prove that very little thing. There's reasons why I can't tell you everything right off the bat, Kid. You can't blame me for sort of soundin' you out an' makin' sure of things, as I go along. I ain't what you think, maybe, but just the same I can do you a good turn an' help my own game, too."

"Where do you want me to ride with you?"

"Down on the Dry Fork!"

The Kid thrilled. It was on the Dry Fork, that bit of sequestered range with its many hiding places, that the rustling operations, for which his foster father had been blamed, had been carried on. Now, Bloomquin wanted him to go down there with him! Was it a trap? If it *was* a trap it was not an ordinary one. He remembered Burkin's warning. But if Bloomquin had wanted his life, he had had ample opportunity to force him into a gun play, or to pot him in the dark. There was something more important than gun play on foot. And Bloomquin was ready to guide him into the very center of things!

"All right, I'll go," suddenly decided The Kid aloud. "When'll we start?"

"Right now, if your horse is handy," said Bloomquin jubilantly.

"He's back here a piece," said The Kid dryly. "You ready?"

"Get your horse, an' I'll be right with you," replied Bloomquin. "We'll go out by the back trail an' swing into the road an' then south."

The Kid marveled that the man should know so much about the lay of the land and the way to the Dry Fork, when he had hardly been in town long enough to gain this knowledge. He wondered, too, about Marcy. He didn't doubt but that Bloomquin had spoken the truth when he said Marcy was not at the cabin, but he assumed that Ben merely had gone into the timber or one of the meadows near the cabin to insure his safety. He speculated as to how long they would be gone, and he remembered he had told Ben he would be back at the cabin that night. Then he reflected that Burkin would in all probability ride up to the cabin and tell Marcy he had gone somewhere with Bloomquin. And Burkin had keen sense enough to suspect their destination. He hummed lightly, as he led the big gray out of the timber.

In a short space he and Bloomquin were threading their way by the back trail to the road. They rode down the gentle grade for a mile, and then The Kid spoke suddenly:

"Whereabouts on the Dry Fork do you want to hit?"

"Whittier's place," replied Bloomquin quickly.

The Kid thrilled again. Whittier's place was well up toward the head of the little creek which threaded its way through the deep cañons, and dried up long before it reached the gentle slopes of the foothills. It was a huge pocket in the limestone walls of one of the most formidable cañons, and once it had been the hiding place and stronghold of a stage robber named Whittier. Because of its inaccessibility and the wild, tumbled ranges about it, it was carefully avoided by stockmen ranging herds in the reserve. Yet The Kid knew a herd could be kept there, for the big amphitheater was carpeted with rich grass, and there was water at that point. They rode for another mile, and then The Kid reined in his horse.

"How far is it to the trail cuttin' in to the south?" he asked.

Bloomquin also pulled up his mount. He looked about them at the fringe of timber along the sides of the road and the dark outlines of near-by ranges above them.

"Maybe I've missed it an' come too far down," he frowned.

The Kid could see his features plainly in the light of the moon which had drifted up over the eastern ridges. It was plain that Bloomquin was not altogether sure of his ground.

"I know a way in, a little piece back," The Kid vouchsafed. "Suppose we go in that way."

Bloomquin readily agreed, and The Kid assumed the leadership. Half a mile back they turned south on a dim trail which barely permitted the passage of their horses, and which they could not easily lose because of the thick stand of pines which hemmed them in on either side.

"You want to ride right in to the Whittier place?" The Kid queried after an hour of steady riding.

"Yes," grunted Bloomquin shortly.

The Kid compressed his lips. The big pocket in the limestone hills was a veritable trap. Once inside a man would have difficulty in getting out of the lower entrance, which was narrow and guarded by sheer cliffs, if those inside wished to prevent him from leaving. And at the upper end was a treacherous trail which was plainly discernible from the floor of the pocket. Otherwise straight walls of rock prevented a hurried exit. It was one of the numerous natural traps for which the queer limestone formation of the Tenderfoot Range was noted.

Silently they rode on, but The Kid was thinking deeply. He wanted to know more about the nature of the expedition before they entered Whittier's Pocket. In the thrill of prospective disclosures he had taken Bloomquin at his word, had accompanied him gladly, for he felt no fear of him alone. He felt he was safe even now, riding along the dim trail ahead of the big man whom he had reason to believe hated him with deadly passion, for he sensed that Bloomquin, despite his blustering confidence, was not familiar with the trails to the Dry Fork and consequently was dependent upon his guidance.

For another two hours they rode their horses at a fast walk. Then The Kid halted on the crest of a tall ridge.

"The Dry Fork is below us," he said quietly.

"An' the Whittier place?" asked Bloomquin eagerly.

"Up the creek a ways," replied The Kid readily.

He sat his horse, eying Bloomquin coolly. Both figures were clearly outlined in the light of the moon which now was nearly overhead.

"Well, let's get goin'," exclaimed Bloomquin impatiently.

"There's a hard trail to follow from here," said The Kid in a quiet voice. "It's steep an' risky. What're we goin' to do when we get down there, Bloomquin?"

"We're goin' to find two men an' about two hundred an' fifty head of stock there an' aroun'. An' you're goin' to show 'em how to get the cattle over the hump without everybody in the country knowin' they're being moved," he added with a knowing look.

The Kid whistled softly. He was watching the big man closely.

"Stolen cattle?" he inquired mildly.

"The same," nodded Bloomquin. "An' the men that's got 'em think I want to buy 'em. I've told 'em they've got to deliver 'em on the other side of the Divide, an' that I'm gettin' you to help 'em over some place besides that main pass where the power line is. Get me?" His thick lips curled in a sneering smile.

"Can't say I do," returned The Kid coldly. "You wantin' me to help you get away with a bunch of rustled cattle?"

"Just that," said Bloomquin quickly. "An' in doin' it we'll get the gang together that did the rustling. When I grab 'em, you'll have your proof that Renault wasn't weedin' out the range hereabouts."

"When you get 'em?" asked The Kid, puzzled.

"Sure," said Bloomquin with a leering smile. "I'm representin' the sheriffs of Musselshell an' Big Falls counties!"

The Kid was looking at him with a searching gaze.

"These men think I've roped you in on the play," said Bloomquin hastily. "They reckon I've got something on you, an' that you're fallin' for a chance to make some easy dough. I knew you an' Marcy had the nerve, an' I knew you knew this country hereabouts—that's why I've asked you in on this deal. You'll clear up the mud aroun' Renault's name an' get a piece of reward money, probably. You're safe with this gang, for they ain't wise to me. You game to go through with it?"

Again The Kid thought hard. Bloomquin's presence with the Musselshell posse, his turning of the Musselshell sheriff from their trail, the presence of Curt Donald, deputy sheriff of Big Falls County, in Jerome, and Bloomquin's reported conference with Ed Mately, all seemed to bear out his statement. But what of the warning Burkin had sounded when he told of what Bloomquin had said to Pinky Swift?

For some time The Kid deliberated. In the end his desire to learn the inside of the rustling operations got the better of his native caution. He'd take a chance. He spurred the big gray and led the way down the perilous trail from the crest of the high ridge.

When they reached the narrow entrance to the Whittier Pocket, he hesitated again, checking his horse. Suddenly rifles cracked from within the entrance, and a number of bullets whistled over their heads.

Bloomquin swore loudly. "They think it's somebody else," he called out, as The Kid was about to whirl his horse and dash for shelter in the timber of the deep slopes on either side of the cañon.

Bloomquin whipped out his gun and fired twice overhead. There were no more shots from the hidden marksmen. The Kid, suddenly suspicious and alert, turned in his saddle to face Bloomquin. He found himself looking into the black bore of the big man's gun. There was a snarling smile of triumph on Bloomquin's lips.

"You're goin' in!" cried the big man, as he motioned with his free hand toward the darkened entrance to the trap.

CHAPTER IX
THROUGH THE SMOKE

With an indefinable look in his eyes The Kid held his right hand aloft, away from his gun, whirled the big gray, and rode swiftly into the narrow passageway leading into the pocket, with Bloomquin close behind him. Two men swung in beside him, as he gained the end of the defile and saw the vast open spaces of the huge cup in the hills which long had served as a rendezvous for bandits in that locality.

It had been here, as The Kid knew, that Mately had found a few head of cattle after Renault's death—cattle which had been left there, while the main herd remained hidden, he suspected. The rustlers had sacrificed those few head to put the stigma of rustling upon Renault and cover their own tracks, so they could continue operations. He had risked everything to make sure of this; now, realizing the trick to which Bloomquin had resorted to get him there, and knowing, too, that he was in grave danger, The Kid became acutely alert, although to all appearances he was cowed and docile—a boy who had been outwitted.

They rode on, with the men at either side of him hazing his horse in the direction they wanted to take, until they came to a two-room cabin near a clump of poplars. The Kid's keen gaze, accustomed to the semi-darkness of the shadowed places in the hills, had sighted the dim shapes of cows and steers toward the upper end of the pocket. He also was surprised that the place was so large. He had visited it but once before, some years past, when no one had been there, although he had many times been on the rim high above the encircling walls of rock.

A light was shining dimly in a window of the cabin, as they dismounted at Bloomquin's order. The Kid followed him inside, with the two others keeping close to him and covering him with their weapons. Inside, The Kid looked curiously about. There was a bunk, a small table, a narrow bench, and two chairs. A door leading into the other room was locked with a padlock. Evidently these quarters had been arranged for his reception.

He stared casually at the two men with Bloomquin and failed to recognize either of them. They were strangers in that country, since he had been away on the other side of the Divide, or they had avoided visiting Jerome, where he would have been almost sure to see them, despite his infrequent visits to town.

"That's all right, you can put up your hardware," Bloomquin was saying gruffly to the pair. "The Kid's come here with me, whether he wanted to or not, an' we'll have that chap, Marcy, here by tomorrow night. I'll see that they turn the trick."

One of the men grinned and winked at Bloomquin. Both seemed to exhibit a certain doubtful respect for The Kid. It was as if he were one of them—with certain reservations. Their manner toward him puzzled him as much as Bloomquin's succession of queer moves made that night.

"I reckon you can beat it," said Bloomquin to the two other men, and then he turned to The Kid.

When he heard the door close after the pair, Bloomquin laid his gun on the table near to his hand and looked at The Kid intently. Suddenly, to the boy's amazement, he broke into a laugh.

"I've got you wonderin'," he smirked. "Ain't I right, Kid?"

"I don't know what your hole card is, Bloomquin," the youth confessed with a scowl. "Don't you reckon you'd better take my gun?"

"Hell, no," boomed the big man. "My play bringin' you in that a way was to impress them two out there. They think I've got you dead to rights, an' I have, so far's that's concerned. But I'm bankin' on you to go through, Kid. I know you're dynamite an' all that, but I take it you'll stick to a game you're liable to get something out of."

He stepped back a pace and deliberately rolled a cigarette which he lighted without looking up. The boy, mystified, was undecided how to take Bloomquin's apparent nonchalance and trust in him. Were the two men outside at each of the two windows? Were there other men guarding the exit out of the pocket? Was Bloomquin pretending to trust him, while holding an ace up his sleeve in that he could prevent his escape?

"It's like this, Kid," Bloomquin resumed. "Now that we're here, we can talk a little plainer. Your pard, Marcy, will be here in a few hours, an' there ain't neither of you goin' out of here till you go to help us drive the cattle over the Divide by some other trail than the main one over the pass south of Milestone. You'd both been here now, if that hadn't been that old fool card sharp with you instead of Marcy. That made me alter my tactics a bit," he added with a chuckle.

"But it's all the same—you've got to come through, whether you want to or not. So look at it sensible, an' there'll be something in it for you. By driving 'em over a secret trail, like these fellers want, we'll get all the bunch together what's workin' on this side. Then, when we meet the other bunch, that I've framed to take the stock on the other side, we'll have both outfits an' rope 'em all in. I'm just makin' sure of your help, because I ain't just sure how you stand."

"An' that's the way you size up to me, Bloomquin," said The Kid. "I ain't sure how *you* stand."

"You've got to take my word for it," the other snapped.

The boy considered this was true. He didn't believe Bloomquin represented the authorities, as he said he did, although there were certain indications which bore out the theory. On the other hand he didn't know if Bloomquin really thought he would help to catch the rustlers, or if he would rather help get away with the cattle and share in a profit.

What was most disconcerting was that The Kid could not be absolutely sure which of these two things the big man wanted to do. But he had discovered the most important thing about the whole business, which was that there were stolen cattle in the pocket, and that the rustlers, with Bloomquin identified with them in some way, were planning to take them over the Divide and wanted his aid as a guide, so the stock could be moved without resorting to the conspicuous trail over the south pass.

The two men who had been with Bloomquin when he accosted The Kid and Burkin, thinking that Burkin was Marcy, undoubtedly had been left in Jerome to capture Marcy and bring him to the pocket.

"You say I've got to take your word for it that you're tryin' to catch these—these boys?" asked The Kid with a gesture toward the outside.

"That's it," beamed Bloomquin. "I see you're beginnin' to show a little sense."

"You been spyin' on 'em, an' you've got it all fixed to rope 'em into a trap?" The Kid continued.

"Bull's-eye," said the other with gusto. "Hit the bell first shot."

"Then you ain't as good as a thief, Bloomquin!" sang The Kid.

He leaped backward, his gun flashing in his hand.

"Don't touch it!" he warned sharply, as Bloomquin reached toward his own weapon, his face purpling.

With a bound The Kid threw the table back against the big man, upsetting the lamp and sending the gun to the floor. He leaped to the outer door and found it locked. There was a flicker of flame, as the oil from the shattered lamp caught fire. Bloomquin was groping behind the upturned table. A bullet from The Kid's gun brought him upright.

"We'll burn, you fool!" he snarled, looking hesitatingly at The Kid and then at the gun on the floor.

The blaze was licking at the table leg and eating into the floor.

The Kid spoke coolly. "Back to the window behind you, Bloomquin, an' keep your back against it. If you don't, I'll let you have it before your men can get here!"

The boy realized that if Bloomquin's men had been at the windows, they would have taken a hand in the game at once—unless they thought they had him trapped. As Bloomquin slowly obeyed, he stepped to one side of the other window, out of range of bullets from that quarter. He faced Bloomquin again, cool and calm, save for a glitter in his eye. The big man's face was twitching in spasms of rage. Curses rumbled in his throat. Then a cunning look came into his eyes which had been darting a red fire of hatred.

"Oh, c'me on, Kid, I was just tryin' you out. I know you're jake. You needn't believe that about me bein' in with the sheriffs. I'll shoot square with you an' see you an' Marcy get your divvy."

"That might make it worse."

Bloomquin showed surprise; then his eyes reddened again with an almost uncontrollable anger.

The fire was gaining headway, and the smoke from the pine table began to choke them.

"You want to burn?" sneered Bloomquin in a voice shaking with rage and derision. "You ain't that big a fool!"

"No, I don't intend to burn, Bloomquin," said The Kid evenly. "I can get through this little window in a jiffy, but it would take you quite a while to squeeze through—maybe you couldn't quite make it, if I didn't give you time enough. They couldn't blame me if you got burned in here. They might never know what became of you, if your men here didn't tell."

Bloomquin was starting with a look of genuine fright. He coughed in the smoke, whereas The Kid, now edging close to the window on his side, was getting better air.

"Bloomquin!" rang the boy's voice. "Tell me, did you know Renault?"

"No!" shouted the man.

"Did you know Spike Harmon, an' did you want to get me for killin' him in a fair gun play?" cried The Kid.

Bloomquin, unable to speak in a paroxysm of coughing, shook his head; but the youth was unable to determine if he shook his head in answer to the question, or to signify that he couldn't talk.

Then Bloomquin, wild with fear and choking with the smoke, turned and pushed out the double pane of glass in the window behind him. He groped blindly for a chair to raise himself on a level with the window, so he could squeeze himself through.

After a moment's hesitation The Kid grasped the other chair and swung it against the pane in the window beside him. He, too, was feeling the ill effects of the smoke, and there was danger that the deadly carbon-monoxide fumes might get them both before they could escape. He began to feel weak in the knees and hurriedly climbed upon the chair. He wriggled through the window and dropped to the ground.

From below in the pocket he heard the pound of hoofs. He made out the forms of his and Bloomquin's horses near the trees and ran for his mount. He raced away from the burning cabin, as two riders came dashing toward him.

Guns popped behind him and bullets sang over his head. He leaned low in the saddle and drove in his spurs, sending the big gray in a wild gallop toward the exit from the pocket. Now he heard a man's agonized screams above the roar of the guns and the firing stopped. Had Bloomquin made it to freedom and safety, or was he burning to death?

The Kid rode madly on down the length of the pocket to the narrow defile between the towering walls of the cañon and dashed through, unmolested, with the screams of pain and terror still ringing in his ears.

CHAPTER X
"YOU'RE YELLOW!"

After his new-found friend, The Kid, had left him in the cabin to go to Jerome on a mysterious mission, Ben Marcy sat for a considerable length of time on a little bench near the door, watching the velvet twilight steal over the hills.

With the coming of darkness he saw that his horse, missing the company of the animal which The Kid had ridden away, had strayed to the lower end of the meadow. Marcy went inside the cabin, took his rope from his saddle, and went out, closing the door. He walked to the lower end of the meadow, intending to lead his horse back to the corral in the rear of the cabin, lest the animal should stray.

When he had fixed the rope to the halter ring he looked up suddenly with an alert gaze and ear. From the trail below he heard a muffled sound—another and another. Then the sounds ceased.

Quickly he led the horse some distance into the thick timber and held its nose to prevent a nicker. He heard no further sounds for some time and, tying his mount, crept through the trees to the edge of the meadow. Then he heard an exclamation in a rough voice.

"They ain't here!"

"They've sloped sure as shootin'," came another voice.

He saw two men coming out of the cabin. There were no horses in the meadow, and he rightly surmised that the men, who evidently were looking for himself and The Kid, had left their mounts in the trail below and had approached on foot to avoid any noise. That showed they had expected to take their quarry by surprise, and Marcy smiled grimly.

"No hosses here either," one of the men was saying.

"They've sloped all right, an' Mort'll be sore as a boil."

"If we hadn't got off the trail we mighta got here in time to head 'em off," said the other. "Mort Bloomquin oughta know we don't savvy this country well enough to hold a strange trail in the dark, when it's no bigger'n a muskrat runway!"

The men continued to mutter, as they looked about

the cabin. Then they came back the length of the meadow and disappeared down the trail. It was too dark for Marcy to get a good look at the pair, but he failed to recognize either voice as one he had ever heard before. He stole to the lower end of the meadow again and listened until he heard the sound of hoofs on the down trail—evidence that the men were going back where they had come from. The fact that they had lost their way explained how they had failed to meet The Kid on his way to town.

Marcy deliberated. He was no fool, and he sensed that the pair had come on some sinister errand. It was certain, however, that The Kid had reached town safely and, unless he was waylaid, could take care of himself. Marcy felt confident of that. Should he attempt to follow the trail into town and tell The Kid of the mysterious visit?

He was pondering this when there came a sudden clatter of hoofs on a west trail, and a rider burst into the clearing from that direction. Marcy had dodged back into the deep shadow of the trees, and he watched this new rider dismount boldly at the door and rap upon it with the butt of a gun. Receiving no answer the man quickly tried the door, flung it open, and entered. A match flared. The man came out, glanced quickly about the confines of the meadow, mounted, and loped to the trail which led to town. He slowed his pace to a walk, as he descended, and finally Marcy heard nothing save the whisper of the wind in the long, shadowy reaches of timber.

Within the shelter of the trees he puzzled over the

advent of this new visitor. Perhaps the man was a friend of The Kid. He had not entered the meadow with stealth and had boldly announced his presence. Indeed to Marcy it seemed that his actions carried a hint of authority. It was a troubling thought.

Marcy groped his way back to his horse and then was struck by another thought. The mysterious visitors might return—or there might be others. He decided it would be the best policy not to spend the night in the cabin and not to put his horse in the corral.

He scouted about until he found a little opening among the trees, and there he tethered his mount. Then he stole to the cabin and got his saddle and slicker pack which he carried to where he had tied his horse. He now was ready for a quick getaway, or to go on The Kid's trail, which he intended to do, if his friend did not put in an appearance before dawn. The Kid had promised to be back before morning.

Marcy waited for a time in the shadows of the timber. Then he again visited the cabin, this time to get a blanket. He spread it on the grass at the edge of the meadow under the trees, near the point where he had his horse, and lay down to rest. The night was warm. He had slept but little the night before, and he soon dropped into a deep slumber. He woke suddenly, sitting bolt upright, and instinctively reached for his gun. He heard a chuckle and, looking behind him, saw a man standing near a horse. Dawn was breaking.

"Boy, you sure was tearing it off," said the stranger with a smile.

He was a gray-haired man, dressed in black. He wore

a drooping mustache, and his features were pleasant, though rather cold.

"My name's Burkin," he announced, as Marcy stared at him. "Has Charley French got back? It don't look like it," he added with a frown.

"Who's Charley French?" asked Marcy.

"Oh, by the way, are you Ben Marcy?" Burkin countered.

Marcy hesitated, but the other's look was reassuring, and he nodded.

"Charley told me you were here," said the old gambler. "I guess you know him as The Spectacular Kid. They fastened that name on him because he's got a fancy for silver trappings an' ornaments on his clothes an' saddle. You been here all night?"

"Yes," said Marcy slowly, as he rose to his feet. "But you ain't tellin' me much about yourself?"

Burkin quickly explained that he was a friend of The Kid's, and when he told about the boy going with Bloomquin, Marcy whistled.

"That don't look good," said Marcy. Then he recounted the advent of the visitors of the night before. Burkin was puzzled.

"I reckon it was the two men who was with Bloomquin an' got the drop on The Kid an' me, that was up here," he reasoned. "They thought I was you. Now they're probably looking for you. The other night rider was Curt Donald, deputy sheriff from the county seat. I don't savvy what he wants with The Kid, an' I don't intend to tell him anything I know.

"Tell you what, Marcy—we'd better slope down to

my place. I've a cabin on a ridge above the road at the upper end of town. I don't figure The Kid is coming back here right away, for he knew I'd get up to see you after what he said when he was goin' away with Bloomquin. If he does show up here an' finds you gone, he'll look me up. Let's beat it before any more riders come along this way."

Ben considered this good advice and went for his horse. They rode down the trail, with Burkin in the lead, and skirted the town to the latter's cabin. There Marcy looked after the horses, while Burkin prepared breakfast.

They ate silently, except for enough casual explanation for each to become acquainted with the other. Marcy was fascinated by the philosophy of the gambler, who was one of the old school—a square card player who depended upon skill. There were few of them left, the boy reflected. Burkin, in turn, was interested in the youth's story of how he had come to meet The Kid and their subsequent adventures.

"Bloomquin let The Kid bluff him out, down there in Dry Crossing, when they first met, because he wanted to use him some way," Burkin said. "An' The Kid made his play to draw the big fellow out. He ain't afraid of him, but I believe, like you say, that Bloomquin's a bad man."

"I'm goin' into town," Marcy announced after the meal.

Burkin shrugged and then withheld his advice to stay away when he saw the look in Ben's eyes. The boy was going to look for his partner—to help him if he needed help. Many times in his own youth the old gambler had done the same thing. He thrilled, and his habitual masked features glowed momentarily, as he again witnessed the spectacle of two young blades adhering to the code of loyalty which had been the very essence of the West.

Ben rode swiftly into town. Because Plank's place was at the extreme eastern end of town, while he rode in from the western end, it was the last resort he visited in his effort to locate his friend. And he was surprised to note, when he entered, that he apparently was known. At least he attracted attention.

One man in particular interested him. This man was standing at the bar with two others, as Ben advanced. He was a florid man, with a shifty blue eye and a mouth filled with gold. Instantly Marcy recalled The Kid's description of Pinky Swift, the tinhorn gambler, and, to his surprise, he found that he had seen this man on two or three occasions in the Musselshell country. As he recalled it, he had seen Swift at shipping time.

Swift and the two men with him were the only men, with the exception of the bartender, in the place at that early hour. It was the lull between first-drink time and the hour when the day's business would begin in earnest. Marcy saw the trio regarding him in the mirror, as he ordered a drink. He proposed to dally with the white liquor and see more of Swift. But Pinky Swift evidently intended to see more of him, also. He turned toward Marcy, as the bartender put out the bottle.

"Ain't askin' us all in?" he said in a voice which sounded friendly.

"Nope," replied Marcy shortly. "Don't happen to be that flush."

All he had in his pocket was a ten-dollar bill which Burkin had insisted on loaning him.

"Then maybe you'd better take one with us," said Swift with a peculiar grin which displayed his gold teeth in vulgar profusion.

"Hate to do that, when I can't blow back," replied Marcy with an inquiring lift of his brows. "Ain't I seen you somewheres before?"

Swift's grin froze. The others became more attentive at this.

"I've been here an' there," said Swift. "Where do you recall seein' me, do you think?"

"'Bout shippin' time once or twice down in the Musselshell country," answered Marcy boldly.

Swift frowned uglily. "Maybe you're bankin' too much on your memory," he flashed. "How'd you come to leave down there?"

Marcy sensed at once that Swift knew about his escape from the Musselshell sheriff. Either the gambler had identified him from the sheriff's description, when that official was in Jerome, or Bloomquin had told him. Suddenly his heart leaped. He believed—yes, he was sure! He had on one occasion seen Swift in Bloomquin's company in the south country! Hadn't The Kid said Swift was in with Spike Harmon, whom he suspected of rustling? And now he had learned that Swift and Bloomquin were connected in some way.

Had Bloomquin come north to take the place of Harmon, the dead chief of the cattle thieves?

His thoughts were interrupted by Swift. "You ain't answered my question!"

"Oh, you got to have an answer," said Marcy, angry, but alert. "Well, I'm like you. I go here an' there."

"Ha! He's tellin' you, Pinky." It was one of the two men with Swift who spoke, and Marcy instantly recognized the voice as that of one of the pair who had visited The Kid's cabin the night before.

His eyes narrowed, as they met Swift's glare of rage.

"I reckon you travel here an' there with more'n one horse, so's to be ready for emergencies, eh?" sneered Swift, his anger getting the better of him.

Marcy became cool. "Maybe so," he said evenly. "Don't you ever pack any spare *stock* along with you?"

It was a dangerous thrust, and it hit its mark. Swift's face purpled with rage.

"You're goin' to put yourself in the same boat with another upstart that's been lording it aroun' here."

"Oh, is he in a boat?" asked Marcy coolly. There was a chance, he decided, that Swift might be taunted into making a slip which would give him an inkling of The Kid's whereabouts.

One of the other men nudged Swift, speaking in an undertone. But the gambler did not take his eyes from Ben's.

"You're fresh," he snarled. "An' you ain't got the guts to go through with anything you start. I knew you was a lemon when you gave up them horses. You're yellow!"

Swift's passion had got beyond his control, and now Marcy's cold anger threatened to dissipate his caution. It was the more tantalizing because he felt certain that Swift knew where The Kid was at that very minute. His face was white and grim. He strove to retain a semblance of composure, but only partly succeeded.

"You ain't keepin' your cards covered up right well, Swift," he said in a low voice which trembled.

The gambler mistook the quaver in his voice, and his agitation for something other than it was.

"You're yellow!" he roared. "What you need is a spanking!"

"Swift—you—lie!" cried Marcy in a shaking voice.

The gambler's thin lips curled back, showing a flash of gold in vivid contrast to his purpled face and the red gleam in his eyes. The sound of a slap broke upon the stillness with the effect of a pistol shot. Marcy staggered back a pace, his left hand whipping up to cover the red splotch on his left cheek. His jaw sagged, then snapped shut with a click, and his lips tightened and showed white. Swift was leering at him with bloodshot eyes. Next instant Marcy's right fist shot out and landed full on the gambler's jaw, knocking him back against his companions with a force which shook the bar.

CHAPTER XI
FISTS AND GUNS

Whatever it was that prompted Pinky Swift to slap Ben Marcy with his open hand instead of going for his gun, also caused Marcy to welcome the opportunity to use his fists. But the man behind the bar, who made no move to interfere, knew the truth. Neither Swift nor Marcy was a gunman. He had known it of Swift for a long time, and he surmised it of Marcy by the youth's actions. But what he and Swift's friends did not know was that neither Swift nor Marcy knew the other was not an expert with a shooting iron.

Swift apparently forgot he had a gun at all, as he swung out from the bar. He had been a prize fighter of sorts in his day, and he had learned many tricks since.

"I'll break you in two!" he gritted between his teeth, as he leaped toward the youth.

His companions stepped back. Marcy met the other's rush with a whirlwind of swings, none of which landed. Then Swift landed on his face, and the blood spurted. Marcy plowed his way into a clinch, and in the break staggered Swift, with a left which knocked him back against a table. The gambler clawed the air and fell against a chair. Marcy bounded upon him, sending him to the floor and smashing the chair into a mass of rungs and splinters.

Then Swift forgot the rules of the roped rings he had known, and instinctively and savagely he adopted the style of the saloons and cow camps, in which his later battles—and all of Marcy's for that matter—had been staged. The two rolled over and over upon the floor, scattering the remnants of the broken chair and over-turning others.

Swift came free and rose with a splinter in his hand. Marcy slid under a table in time to avoid the missile which split the table top, as if it had been made of card-board. There had been death in the vicious power behind that blow.

Marcy knew that he was fighting for his life; he could see the lust to kill in Swift's eyes, and, even though he himself was in the throes of a great passion, he marveled in a flashing interval, as he sprung out from the shelter of the table, that his veiled intimation that Swift might be associated with the rustlers, should drive the gambler to strive to do away with him.

Swift came lunging toward him. There was a wary, calculating light in his eyes. He began to spar and use footwork, kicking two of the card tables out of the way. But in this he was no match for the younger man, who was faster on his feet. Swift had the advantage of weight, but Marcy was speedier, and the boy's muscles were hard as steel from months of toil on the open range.

Marcy darted in and whipped home a stinging right to his opponent's jaw. It was the third time he had hit that spot, and Swift swung viciously, wild with fury. Then Marcy determined to try to wear his heavier adversary out. Already Swift was showing the effects of his inactive life and enervating habits. He was beginning to puff; wise in ancient ring experience, he recognized the danger sign and plunged in again, taking a rain of blows, and went into a clinch.

The two crashed to the floor. Marcy soon learned that Swift knew something of wrestling, and how to use his strength to best advantage. He intended to wear Marcy out by sheer excess of weight.

Swift's two companions were yelling encouragement to him. They believed the gambler had the advantage and were shouting instructions. As they thrashed about the floor, Swift trying to secure a telling hold, and Marcy twisting out of danger time after time, the boy felt a hard object against his back, as he fought the gambler off. He knew it was a gun! Like Swift, he had forgotten his gun, and now he wondered if it had dropped out of its holster, as was likely, or if it was Swift's gun which was on the floor.

The realization that he might be unarmed, if it should come to a duel with weapons, lent him added strength, and, with an almost superhuman effort, he threw Swift off and squirmed free. In that flashing instant his hand flew to his side. His holster was empty!

A jeer of derision went up from Swift's companions.

"He was goin' for his cannon!" yelled the voice which Marcy had recognized.

Swift's arm flashed out, as he rose, and Marcy dropped, when a missile whizzed over his head. A crash of breaking glass against the foot rail of the bar told Marcy that the gambler had thrown a bottle which he had found on the floor. He plunged in again, his eyes narrowed to mere slits, his face pale and dripping crimson. This time Swift did not ward off his blows with his former strength and skill. He was tiring fast. Yet Marcy could not get in the blow which would end the battle. Swift took to covering up and giving ground. He backed around in a circle, sparring for a chance to recover his wind. His look of cunning had come again into his eyes. Marcy sensed that he was planning a change of tactics; but he didn't fully realize the significance of Swift's purpose in running before him.

Suddenly the gambler darted out of range, as Marcy hung motionless for an instant, after another vigorous try for Swift's jaw. Stepping behind a table, his eyes lit by savage fury, his face livid and his breath coming in sobbing gasps, Swift nevertheless managed to sneer. He attempted to speak, but his words died in his throat, inarticulate. There was a sudden hush in the shouts of his companions. Then Marcy divined the gambler's purpose, as he noted that the butt of a gun protruded from Swift's holster, the flap of which was pinned down. Swift intended to disregard the fact that Marcy was unarmed.

It would not take Swift long to get his gun out; but it would take him longer than it would if the holster flap was loose or missing. Marcy waited, gathering his muscles, his eyes burning into Swift's. In that incalculable instant, when Swift started for his gun, Marcy leaped forward, literally scooping a chair from the floor.

Swift's gun was popping from the unbuttoned holster, as Marcy threw the chair with all his strength and hurled himself to the floor, as it shot from his hand. It struck Swift in the chest and arm, staggering him and checking his draw. The pistol barked, and a bullet harmlessly splintered the edge of the table. From underneath, Marcy made a flying tackle, and the table rode on his back, as his arms clasped Swift's legs below the knees. Swift toppled backward, firing aimlessly again. Marcy loosed his hold and shook himself free from the table. Swift, raising himself on his elbow, whipped his weapon into aim in his right hand.

In the instant's pause Marcy heard the front door open. He swung his right foot in a vicious kick, aimed at Swift's right hand, just as the gun roared. The kick knocked the gambler's hand and arm up, as the bullet sped on its way, and the toe of Marcy's boot caught Swift just under the jaw.

Marcy felt a shock in his left arm, and then it dangled, numb and useless at his side. Swift dropped back flat on the floor and lay motionless.

"Drop it!" Marcy heard a familiar voice call out, like the crack of a whip. Then the world suddenly tumbled about him with a crash and was blotted out by blackness deeper than the deepest inky void of night.

The man who had struck Marcy on the head with the butt of his six-shooter whirled about. Near the door stood a youth, white-faced and grim, his eyes glinting with a steel-blue flame. In his hand at his hip was a pearl-handled gun.

"The Kid!" exclaimed the man who had struck Marcy, while his companion raised his hands over his head.

"Drop it, or start to use it!" cried The Kid sternly.

The man hesitated an instant, his face twitching, the fingers of his free hand opening and closing spasmodically. Then with a sneer he dropped the gun, and it rattled dully on the floor. The Kid walked quickly past them and, without taking his gaze from them, picked up the senseless form of Ben Marcy and backed with it to the door. He paused a moment, the sun gleaming brightly on the silver trappings on his holster and gauntlets.

"If either of you gents slips your head out of this door, it'll stop hot lead," he called back sternly.

He passed through the door, stuck his gun in its holster, and ran with Marcy in his arms around the corner of the building to the big gray which was standing near the trees. He threw Marcy across the saddle, mounted behind him, and spurred Ironsides into a trail leading into the timber. He called to the big horse, raking his flanks with his steel, and the magnificent beast, realizing that he was called upon to carry a double burden and perform his best, responded by galloping up the trail in great lunges which called for every iota of strength in his muscles and heart.

Where Marcy's horse was, The Kid did not know or care. His brain was in a tumult. He knew by some latent but overpowering instinct that Marcy had got into trouble with Swift in an effort to locate him, The Kid. He thanked his stars he had arrived from the Dry Fork in time. He thought he had recognized the strangers with Marcy as the two men who had been with Bloomquin the night before. Perhaps they had planned to lay Marcy out and take him to the Whittier Pocket, a captive. Bloomquin had expected them to do it. He could have killed them both with relish, when he saw the gun descended upon Marcy's head. Now he was glad he had not done so.

A low moan came from Marcy's lips. The Kid had twisted the bridle reins about the saddle horn and was holding on by keeping Marcy in the saddle. Now he leaned forward, holding Marcy with one hand, while he secured the reins and checked the big gray; presently he turned him into a dim path leading directly northward over the ridges.

The jack pines growing close to the narrow trail caught at Marcy's hands and legs, and The Kid felt a splash on his hand. He gasped as he saw that Marcy was bleeding. A little opening appeared in the timber. It was the bottom of a shallow draw, with a thin ribbon of a mountain stream flowing through it. The Kid pulled up the panting gray, slid down, and eased Marcy out of the saddle. He laid him down upon the soft grass near the water.

For a few brief moments he listened intently, but could hear no sounds of pursuit. He was off the worn network of trails. Now he bent over Marcy and opened his shirt with trembling fingers. As he did so, Marcy moaned again. The Kid sighed with relief when he failed to find a wound in Ben's breast. Then Marcy opened his eyes. He stared up at The Kid.

"Hello," he whispered faintly.

"Where are you hit, Ben?" asked The Kid anxiously.

"Head—arm—left arm—head feels awful—water."

The Kid took out his knife and cut away the sleeve about Ben's left arm. After a quick examination he smiled.

"That ain't so bad," he said cheerfully, while Marcy tried to smile back at him. "I guess your head feels worse, eh? One of those hombres rapped you with the butt of his gun."

Fetching some water in his hat he gave Marcy a drink. Then he poured some on his aching head, and tearing off his own scarf, he soon had the wound in the fleshy part of Marcy's left arm tightly bandaged. In a short time Marcy was sitting up. He drank much water, and The Kid constantly bathed his head. He tried to talk, but The Kid stopped him.

"Plenty of time to talk when we get where we're goin'," he said, as he helped Marcy into the saddle and then mounted behind him.

They rode easier this time, for Marcy found he could cling to the saddle horn with his right hand. His left arm was in a sling improvised from his scarf.

"Where we bound for?" he asked curiously.

"Home, I reckon," replied The Kid with a whimsical note in his voice.

Then he turned into a trail which led up the mountain ridges toward the secret pass on the north shoulder of Milestone Peak and the rendezvous in the flower-splashed meadow near Tenderfoot Falls.

CHAPTER XII
A DESPERATE MOVE

Three times they halted among the fragrant pines beside a spring or trickling stream before they reached the last steep pitch of the secret trail. Here The Kid dismounted to ease the burden on the big horse. Marcy insisted that he felt strong enough to sit in the saddle without assistance. Thus they proceeded up the final slope to the little-known pass over the north shoulder of the peak.

In the lap of the pass they rested. On either side the high, rock-ribbed ridges fell away down the long slopes toward the distant foothills, while north and south of them ranged the wind-blown crest of the Divide, bare of timber, strewn with granite outcroppings—desolate, yet weirdly and wildly beautiful.

The Kid told Marcy of his adventures with Bloomquin on the Dry Fork, and in turn he heard what had happened that morning in Jerome.

"They figured on puttin' you out an' hustling you down to the Whittier place," he told Marcy. "That's what Bloomquin left that pair up there for. But Pinky—I reckon he was mad clear through an' wanted to get you right. I guess I'd have killed him, if I'd got in when he first pulled that gun. Lucky I got there when I did. I had to ride pretty hard back from the Dry Fork an' then up here. Ben, there ain't another horse in the country that can stand what Ironsides can. Renault got him; an' he said he was the best horse he ever saw."

The Kid continued to walk, when they started on. The afternoon was drawing to a close in gold and crimson glory, as they heard the faint roar of the Falls. Soon after they entered a long meadow with a cabin, barn, and corrals at its upper end.

"Remember what I told you," The Kid cautioned.

He had warned Marcy not to speak of their adventures, or to tell the girl, whom he would see here, anything about The Kid's past experiences, or the killing of Harmon. These were things which he did not want the girl to know, although her father, John Reynolds, who had known Renault and The Kid for years, was in possession of all the facts. They had not progressed far across the meadow when a white gleam showed in the doorway of the cabin, and a girl came running out.

As they approached, The Kid walking ahead of the horse bearing Marcy, she came slowly toward them. Her face lighted and flushed prettily under her golden hair, as she looked at The Kid. Then she looked at Marcy wonderingly and with a show of concern. Marcy could not help but stare at her, and she flushed again. Something within The Kid stirred; but he quickly put the thought out of his mind when she spoke to him.

"Charley! You're—you're back again!"

The light in her eyes brought back the joyous feeling in his heart.

"An' got a sort of cripple with me, Lettie," he said, reaching for her hands. "This is Ben Marcy. He got accidently shot in his left arm, an' I brought him over

94

here to rest up a day or two. It gave me a good excuse to visit you," he concluded with a boyish laugh.

"You don't need any excuses to visit me, Charley French," she said, and then caught herself with another blush. The Kid stepped to the horse just in time to prevent Marcy from falling in his effort to dismount.

"Guess that right arm ain't as strong as I always thought it was," said Marcy in a tired voice. Loss of blood and the blow upon his head had weakened him.

"We'll get you to the cabin," said The Kid, taking him by his good arm and helping him to the doorway.

John Reynolds came hurrying from the barn. Without waiting for an explanation he helped The Kid put Marcy on a couch in the little sitting room of the cabin.

"Get some warm water, Lettie, an' see if you can put a regular bandage on his arm," he told his daughter. "I'll get him a little bracer, an' then he better have some coffee an' a little to eat."

He didn't ask The Kid for details. He gave the impression that, regardless of who Marcy was, or how he came to be wounded, the fact that he was there with Charley French, The Kid, was enough. And Marcy remembered that The Kid had called this "home."

As the girl was tenderly dressing Marcy's wound, while Ben looked at her in undisguised admiration, The Kid again felt that disturbing feeling within him. Once he frowned.

John Reynolds saw it and grinned.

When Marcy had had his drink of the good liquor— which Reynolds had saved for emergencies—and had been fed and put to bed in the small room which constituted the left wing of the cabin, The Kid told the old man what had happened, lowering his voice so that the girl in the kitchen could not hear.

"Is Bloomquin badly hurt or dead, do you know?"

"I don't know for sure," replied The Kid, "but I don't think so. He was stuck in that window and scared with the fire licking his heels, I reckon. His men could get him out, an' his face was outside the window, so he could get good air."

Reynolds deliberated, then shook his head.

"I don't think he's connected with any sheriff's office by what you tell me," he said; "but I can't figure what Curt Donald is doin' down here."

"There ain't nothin' I know of he'd be lookin' for me for," said The Kid, puzzled. "He knows me, of course, from the time I raided that joint in Alder Park an' got back the money you'd been cheated out of at cards.

"But he shot square an' turned me loose when he heard the facts," The Kid continued. "He's the best officer in these parts, I'll say; an' now that he's aroun' here you can bet all the blue checks he ain't aroun' for nothin'."

"Mately's been letting Jerome run pretty wide an' handsome," Reynolds reflected aloud. "Maybe talk of the doin's there had leaked into the county seat an' set the sheriff to thinkin' it'd help him to clean up 'fore election."

"What are you two talkin' about?" pouted Lettie Reynolds, coming in from the kitchen.

"Why, Charley here was just tellin' me he wanted to

take a walk with you, so's he could say howdy, good an' proper," replied her father with a laugh.

The Kid and the girl reddened.

"Father, you're getting fresh," said Lettie.

But a few minutes later The Kid and the girl were walking in the fragrant meadow under the blossoming stars.

"Charley, how did your friend really get shot?" Lettie asked.

He knew the question was coming, and he had been talking lightly of everything and anything in an effort to stall it off. But the girl's curiosity was roused.

The Kid did not want to tell her of the reputation he had unavoidably earned as a gunman. He did not want to worry her with a recital of all that had happened to him since the death of his foster father. He particularly did not want to tell of this latest trouble, for to do so would cause her to look with suspicion upon Ben Marcy, even though her father would in the end convince her that both he and Marcy were not as they had been painted. He paused in the starlight and took both her hands.

"Lettie, do you trust me?" he asked in a low voice.

"Why, Charley! What a silly question!" Her real answer was in her eyes, and his heart bounded.

"Listen, girlie," he cried softly, seizing her in his arms; "I can't tell you everything—not now. There's too much to tell. You wouldn't understand it all. I'm goin' to tell you enough of the truth so you'll know I'm in earnest."

He held her tightly, and she looked up into his eyes.

"Ben Marcy was shot by a man because he was tryin' to help me," whispered the boy. "If I tell you why he was tryin' to help me, I've got to tell you a long story, sweetheart. It's too long an' too soon to tell you now. But I promise you I'll tell you everything when it's all over, if you'll promise to wait till then an' not to worry."

"Are you in danger, Charley?"

"Not in the way you might think," he evaded. "Everything will come out all right, girlie. Will you trust me an' promise not to worry or ask me about anything till—till I come to you to tell you?"

For answer she gave him her lips.

Ben Marcy was much better next day. He went down to the stream with The Kid and watched enthusiastically, while his friend caught a mess of native trout. They had them for supper, and Lettie favored both youths with her smile.

The Kid felt the nameless thing within him stir again. Ben Marcy was good-looking. He had not told Ben that he and Lettie Reynolds had had an understanding, and that a certain event was expected to be celebrated along about Christmas time, if things went well with him. He caught himself up sharply, as he looked jealously on, while the girl dressed Marcy's wound. And again that night he forgot his misgivings, when he and Lettie walked in the light of the stars. Next day at noon they were startled by the sound of hoofs.

As The Kid's hand dropped instinctively to his gun, John Reynolds left the table and hurried outside. The girl looked frightened, when she saw the look in The Kid's eyes and Marcy's alertness. Then The Kid heard a familiar voice and went out. It was Burkin, and he was leading Ben Marcy's horse.

"How'd you know we was here?" demanded The Kid.

"Renault had often told me in confidence about this place, where he used to keep his spare horses," smiled Burkin. "I reckoned you might be here. It's the first time I ever came up that trail, an' it's the toughest I ever hit yet."

The Kid introduced him to John Reynolds and led the horses away. When Burkin had eaten, he went out to the shade of an alder near the corral, replying slowly to The Kid's eager questions and listening to the boy's account of what had happened at the Whittier place.

No, Bloomquin hadn't shown up in town, an' he hadn't been reported dead or hurt. Burkin believed that, while the big man was a gun expert and all that, he would show the yellow feather in the face of death from any other cause than by violence. The two men who had been with Pinky Swift had disappeared. Curt Donald had ridden out of town on the road to the Basin, without giving any information to any one about his mission.

Marcy now spoke up. "I've seen that feller Swift in the Musselshell country along about shippin' time," he said stoutly; "an' I saw him with Bloomquin, I know. You say he was a pal of this rustler, Spike Harmon? Well, I'll bet he was the one that engineered the sale of the stock that Harmon an' his crowd got away with.

An' I'll bet he sold 'em to Bloomquin down there, an' that Bloomquin handled the business from that end. Now that Harmon got killed this spring, I'll bet my hoss an' saddle that Bloomquin's up here to take charge of the stock they've rustled this summer. Didn't a lot of the crowd that was with Harmon slope out when he was killed?"

Both The Kid and Burkin nodded.

"Then that's why they wanted you to show 'em how to get the cattle out over the Divide an' down Smith River by a trail aside from that one over the main pass," said Marcy in triumph to The Kid. "They didn't have much trouble gettin' the stock together an' workin' the brands, but they ain't got anybody in with 'em that knows the country well enough to take charge of the drive to market!"

John Reynolds agreed with Marcy.

"Well, I know what I'm goin' to do," said The Kid in a determined voice. "I'm goin' to make Pinky Swift talk! I made him tell how Harmon killed Fred Renault, an' if I could make him talk once I'll make him talk again!"

"No, you'll never make Pinky Swift talk again," said Burkin soberly.

"What's that?" flared The Kid. "Why not?"

"Because Pinky Swift is dead!" Burkin announced.

There was a moment of silence broken only by Marcy's heavy breathing.

"Then they're lookin' for me?" asked Ben.

"No, I don't think so," said the old gambler. "Of course your kick hurried Swift's demise along, I expect; but Pinky's been goin' against the white likker pretty strong, an' his heart was none too good. His passion of rage an' the hard exercise he indulged in with you is what got him, I reckon. Anyway they don't know where you are, an' the two that was with him lit out right after it happened. The only witness is the bartender, you might say, for they mightn't go much by what The Kid saw, an' the bartender sort of admires the fight you put up, an' he thinks Pinky had it comin' to him for tryin' to shoot you down when you didn't have a gun."

Marcy breathed easier, but he still was a prey to grave fears.

"There's just one thing left for me to do," said The Kid in sudden decision. "I'm goin' to find Curt Donald, an' put the whole business up to him, straight from the shoulder."

As the others stared at him, he left them and walked away by himself to think.

Burkin went back that afternoon. The Kid avoided the girl. He knew she was struggling with an overpowering desire to demand the truth from him. And he knew that, if she asked him again, he would have to tell her everything—that he had killed, that his foster father was suspected and accused of being a rustler, that he, himself, was believed by many to have been implicated in shady deals. And what could he prove?

When he returned to the cabin in the late afternoon, after a session with his thoughts, and saw Ben and Lettie chatting gayly and laughing together, the thing

101

which gripped his heart caused him to frown. He was silent at supper.

After the meal he saddled the big gray, and replying casually to the questions and advice of John Reynolds and Marcy, he led the horse out of the corral and mounted. He waved to the girl and galloped away without further farewell.

The big gray made splendid time after his period of rest. It was only two hours after dark when they topped the Divide and began the descent by the secret trail.

The Kid was determined to see Curt Donald. Was Bloomquin still in the pocket on the Dry Fork? He could readily see why it would be advantageous for the rustlers to take their stolen stock out now. It had been a dry season, and much stock had been moved out of the Basin to other ranges. This had taken men, and the cattle in the reserve had not been watched as carefully as usual. The rustlers had had ample opportunity to work unmolested. But they would have to get their stock out before the men came into the hills to drive out the cattle there. By taking out the stolen cattle now they would avoid the round-up and could take advantage of the early market for prime beef.

Suddenly The Kid's thoughts were interrupted by a strange sight. As he came out upon the crest of a ridge above the town of Jerome, the long curve of the hills to southward was suddenly revealed. But instead of the dark shadow of the forests and the hulk of the range against the star-filled sky, which The Kid expected to see, he saw a ruddy glow which sent fingers of red creeping up into the sky.

A forest fire? No, a forest fire would hardly make such a concentrated blaze. The Kid turned along the crest of the ridge and picked his way southward. The ruddy flare increased, and flames shot up against the inky background. Then The Kid located it.

The Jericho mine buildings above Jerome on the south were burning! He drove in his spurs and galloped along a trail leading to the main trail over the Divide from where he could gain the road leading to the mines. When he reached a point over the trail to the pass, he reined in his mount and sat staring in astonishment. Below he could see the shadowy shapes of moving cattle.

At first thought he wondered if they were range cattle fleeing from the fire. But, no, there were no cattle being ranged in the tumbled section about the mines which were located at the head of the Dry Fork.

Suddenly the appalling significance of the sight he witnessed was borne in upon him. Bloomquin was carrying out a desperate scheme. He doubtless had set fire to the mine buildings to draw attention to Jericho. Every man in Jerome would hasten up there to help fight that fire, for the Jericho pay roll meant much to Jerome. And with every man's attention riveted on the fire, and the main trail cleared of stragglers, Bloomquin was deliberately driving the stolen herd up to the main pass across the Divide!

CHAPTER XIII
THE WHITE LIGHT

His first thought was to go for help—to sound a warning. But there were certain drawbacks to this plan. In the first place he knew that every man who could get there had gone from Jerome to the Jericho to help fight the fire. And to get to the mine would take some time, from his present position. Moreover there were many who would not believe him, even if they would take time to listen, and more who would not care to interfere with the supposed rustlers. And he doubted if it would be reasonable to ask them to stop fighting the fire and endeavor to capture the cattle thieves.

Those inclined to aid would point out that time would be required to get away with the cattle, after they had been taken across the Divide, and that it would not be hard to catch up with the rustlers, for it was true that the stock could not be driven any distance without a disastrous loss of weight, a result the thieves would wish to avoid, if they planned to market the cattle soon. When the beeves had been driven across the Divide, it would be necessary to graze them down to the shipping point.

But The Kid knew that Bloomquin would probably split the herd into bands and separate the cattle. Also, when they were in the valley west of the range, they could have ample warning of pursuit and make a getaway with ease. Doubtless Bloomquin had figured all this out. And who could prove that he had fired the mine buildings?

The Kid wanted to keep the cattle east of the Divide, where there could be no doubt as to where they had come from, and he wanted to be able to prove who had them in charge. By doing this he would clear the name of his foster father, Renault, of the rustling charges and vindicate himself. It would show up, once and for all, the rustling ring which had been operating in the Tenderfoot foothills adjacent to the Basin for many years.

All this reasoning occupied but a brief space, while the boy watched the shadowy procession of stolen beef passing below him. He saw riders, too, but could not distinguish one from the other.

How was he to stop the herd? He could hardly expect to turn back the cattle and fight off the rustlers, single-handed. Yet in that emergency and with the limited time at his disposal, he could not hope to get help before the stock could be taken over the pass. Already the vanguard of the herd was well on its way up to the last steep stretch of trail leading to the pass. Once over, the going would be easier, and the cattle could be got down almost into the Smith River valley by daylight. And daylight—dawn—would be too late!

Swiftly The Kid thought. If he could turn the cattle back, the identification, and perhaps the capture, of the rustlers, might follow. And the place where he would have the best chance of stopping the herd and flinging it back upon its drivers would be at the eastern end of the pass, just at the top of the last steep pitch of trail.

He turned the big gray down the ridge, picking a trail leading westward at random. He followed this for some distance at as fast a pace as he could ride with any measure of safety and surety, and then he swung off on a bypath toward the main trail. He now could hear the herd below him. He could hear, too, an occasional shout from the men. The cattle were not moving very fast, he reflected with a grim smile; for cattle are hard to move at night. Also he knew it would take heroic and unusual methods to turn them about and stampede them, as he hoped to do.

At some distance above the herd, he rode into the trail, rounded a bend, and was quickly out of sight, so far as the rustlers were concerned. He doubted if they had seen him in the semidarkness. When he heard nothing from below to indicate that they had, he rode on up the trail which was becoming steeper and steeper.

Bloomquin's assertion that he was connected with the sheriff's offices of two counties, he did not believe, although the arrival of Curt Donald had caused him to ponder. But Donald's business evidently was in the Basin, for he had gone down there the day after he arrived in Jerome, according to Burkin. What influence Bloomquin had used to turn the Musselshell sheriff back in his search for Marcy he did not know; but he believed the big man had promised the official to deliver Marcy to him later. As for Bloomquin's plan with regard to himself, The Kid now saw that Bloomquin had tried to enlist his help in getting the cattle away, and had likely intended to do away with him, after he had taken advantage of his knowledge of the hills.

Obviously this conviction did not serve to put The Kid in a pleasant mood. He remembered Bloomquin's occasional glares of almost insane rage directed at him, and the subsequent attempts to conceal the real nature of his feelings. There could be no doubt but that Bloomquin hated him, and he did not discount the danger which lurked within that hatred. The big gray gained the eastern end of the pass in a mighty spurt of speed, and The Kid reined him in at one side of the narrow depression in the backbone of the ridge which formed the summit of the Divide.

The herd was coming on up the last steep bit of trail, nearer and nearer. He could plainly hear the shouts of the men, and they carried a note of exultation. The rustlers were jubilant because they had got the cattle out of the Dry Fork hiding place, past Jerome and up to the Divide, without being seen, as they thought. Doubtless they had crossed the cattle over the road at a point halfway between the mines and the town, at a time when scouts found the road clear of riders in both directions, and none would think of coming up the trail to the pass, while the fire was raging. It had been a clever, if costly, ruse, and it threatened to succeed, unless The Kid could turn back the cattle.

It could hardly be done by shooting and yelling; for that would bring a fusillade from the rustlers and was liable to send the herd thundering through the pass. But it was apparently the only thing he could do, and he decided to chance it. At best, if he failed, he could retreat and harry the rustlers until dawn, thus slowing up the movement of the herd.

He edged his horse out into the center of the pass, and suddenly the big gray gave a leap. The Kid felt something slap with a sting against his arm. His horse lunged again before his rider could determine what was wrong. Then The Kid spoke to his mount, patted him on the neck to calm him, and dismounted. He found that the gray had stepped into a tangle of wire which had been left in the pass by the men who had wired the high-tension line. The Kid disengaged the wire from about the horse's forelegs, and then he stiffened and looked up at the taut wires overhead, strung between towers at the eastern and western ends of the pass.

In fascination he stared at the three heavy wires. Each of those wires, he understood, carried a hundred and fifty thousand volts. It was the power which was transported across the range to run trains over the Rockies, far to the westward. But it was not of the tremendous power that The Kid thought.

He remembered the crash and the terrific blaze of light which had occurred on two occasions, when he had seen lightning strike these wires down in the foothills. He remembered the blinding glare and steel-blue shafts of light which shot into the sky, when a short circuit had been formed one winter in a way which never had been ascertained. These reflections gave him a great idea.

In his hand he held some wire of the same strength as that which was carrying the heavy voltage above him. The pound of hoofs from the herd was now a mild thunder. Soon the vanguard of the cattle would be upon him. He swiftly took his lariat from his saddle. Throwing it on the ground with the wire he leaped in the saddle and galloped to the western end of the pass. There he left his horse and ran as fast as he could back to where he had left the wire and the lariat.

There was not much of the wire, and it was not heavy. It was clumsy to handle, however, because it was twisted. The Kid hurriedly straightened it out as much as possible. Then he ran to the steep slope up the ridge of the eastern end of the pass. Up and up he climbed and scrambled until he had reached a point halfway between the lap of the pass and the high-tension wires. He hurriedly tied the loose wire to the end of his rawhide lariat. Then he waited in breathless excitement, while the herd came up the last bit of trail below the pass.

Shaking out the noose of his lariat, he whirled it with his right hand, while he held the loosened coils in his left. The wire dangled free of obstructions at his feet. The whirling loop hissed like a snake in the air, as the first shadowy forms of the driven steers showed at the lip of the pass. Then The Kid shot the loop from his right hand.

No sooner had the wire jerked into the air than he leaped in reckless bounds down the steep slope for the bottom of the pass. The rope flew upward, above the wires and out over them. Then it wavered and started to fall. The loop and the long trail of rope hit the second wire, dragging the loose wire to which it was tied. Another barest instant, and there came a series of reports of deafening thunder. Then night was turned to brightest day, as a great shaft of steel-blue light shot into the sky. The tangle of wire which The Kid had tied to the lariat, had formed an arc between two of the high-tension wires, and hundreds of thousands of volts of electricity were turned into a celestial incandescent which lighted all of the dim reaches of the mountains in a blinding glare.

The Kid saw the cattle stop, crowd back, turn. He ran toward them shouting, as they plunged down the steep slope in a stampeding mass, maddened by the unexpected thunder, frightened by the blinding, shooting lights of the arc over the wires.

Then a figure loomed from one side of the slope and came plunging toward him. In a white light, brighter than day, The Kid saw the livid features of Bloomquin distorted by an insensate rage. He had replaced his gun in his holster, and now he stood motionless, as Bloomquin came on. He was awed, fascinated, stupefied by the man's look of brutal, uncontrollable fury. Bloomquin was almost foaming at the lips in the violence of his wrath. Murder—a burning, savage lust to kill—shone red in his eyes. His lips quivered in an effort to speak, but only a croak came from his throat. He bared his teeth in a hideous snarl.

"I'll—pay you!" he managed to get out in a tone that ended in a shriek. "You little rat of hell!"

He came to a stop a few paces from The Kid. Then the boy recovered.

"If you'll stop to think, Bloomquin, you'll remember

I never offered to help you get away with those cattle," he cried sternly. "I know now who was behind Harmon in the rustling you tried to blame on others."

"An' you got Harmon," screamed Bloomquin. "You got him because he wasn't as good a man as me. We'll see pretty quick how fast that Renault crook taught you to draw! I'm here to make you pay—d'ye hear me? To make you pay—an' now!"

The man's eyes burned into the boy's, with an unholy, leering light. The white light from the burning arc made his face seem ghostly and fiendish. Somehow, though he could not see them, the boy sensed the presence of others. Then two right forearms and wrists moved faster than lightning could streak across the sky.

Darkness came, as if the movement was a signal. The overburdened wires had burned out. But two jets of fire split the inky void, as two guns barked as one. The Kid swung half around to the left and staggered back. Another jet of fire flashed low before him. He wondered that it could be so dark, so terribly dark. He heard some one running toward him.

Then the blackness that followed the abrupt shutting off of the arc began to thin, and he dimly saw a heap on the ground before him in the lap of the pass. It seemed to him that he stood there for hours, swaying—rocking, as though in a boat at sea. He felt numb, deliciously tired. He was drifting, and the darkness was coming again. He could no longer see the heap on the ground, or the stars, or the faint outlines of the rock walls of the pass. Something touched his back and shoulder He leaned against it wearily. Sounds of voices, as from a long distance, came to his ears in a murmur like the murmur of the wind in the aisles of the forest. He sighed and gently drifted into unconsciousness.

CHAPTER XIV
THE BROWN ENVELOPE

It was the second morning following his collapse in the pass, when Charley French opened his eyes and looked about intelligently, although a bit bewildered. For hours and hours he had tossed in wild delirium before sleep had come. Then his brow had cooled, and the physician had told the watchers at his bedside that the crisis was over. They might maintain the vigil, if they wished, but he was going to sleep for about ten hours.

When The Kid awoke, he first saw a white muslin curtain fluttering in a breeze. Sunlight was peeping into the room, and through the curtain he could see the green of the poplars. He turned his head on the pillow and looked into the eyes of Lettie Reynolds. That was a good thing, he thought; it was nice to see Lettie standing there above him. And when she leaned over suddenly, after a breathless pause, and kissed him lightly on the lips, he decided that everything was quite all right, despite the fact that he felt strangely weak, and that his left shoulder was encased in bandages.

"You mustn't try to talk," the girl cautioned, putting

a cool finger on his mouth and smoothing his hair. "I'll tell the doctor you're awake and see what he says. Now promise you won't move. Nod your head."

He nodded and was surprised that it was an effort to do so. The doctor let him have a little something to sip that day—some broth that Lettie made—and then took himself off for Jerome. He was the Jericho mine doctor.

That night Curt Donald came into the room and sat quietly by the sick bed. He did not look at The Kid much, but seemed to be doing considerable thinking. Finally he got up to leave.

"So long, Charley," he said quietly, grasping The Kid's free hand for a moment. "I'll probably see you again."

Something in the deputy sheriff's voice made the boy feel glad. Next afternoon Ben Marcy and Burkin were in to see him. He was much better, and he had insisted on talking to Lettie and her father that morning.

"Now what all happened?" The Kid demanded.

"Well, you busted up the rustlin' gang proper," said Burkin. "Bloomquin's dead, an' the rest of the bunch went to the county jail. Now don't get excited, and I'll tell you all you need to know about it now, an' then you can get some more sleep."

Marcy stood looking on.

"Donald came back the afternoon before the fire," said Burkin. "After the fire started I was late gettin' on my way to the Jericho, an' I saw the cattle comin', when I took a short cut from my place. I hustled up an' told Donald, who was at the fire. He got Mately an' two others and went back with me. We followed the herd an' got up there in time to fill a couple of the rustlers with lead an' capture three more. You did for Bloomquin, an' it was a good riddance. It's a wonder he didn't get you. If that bullet in your shoulder had been a little lower, we'd be at the cemetery instead of here."

He frowned in mock severity.

"I might add that one of the men squealed when he saw the jig was up. Donald promised to make it light for him. He said Bloomquin set fire to the mine buildings to cover up his moving the cattle. He'd been in with Spike Harmon an' Pinky Swift, so Renault's record is all clear."

The Kid smiled happily.

"Donald came over to a stockmen's meeting in the Basin, when they asked him to find out who was rustling cattle in the Tenderfoot country. The Basin cattlemen's association offered a thousand dollars to anybody who caught a rustler, an' Donald says you an' Marcy here will come in for a piece of change. Now that's all for now, except that this young lady here"— he pointed to Lettie Reynolds—"has been crying her eyes out for fear you'd die, so I guess you'd better go to sleep an' get well."

An hour later The Kid went to sleep, with the girl's hand in his.

Followed a week of speedy recovery, with the hills taking on the golden garment of autumn. The round-up got under way, and a sun-burned cowpuncher came to the cabin, with a large brown envelope which, when opened, was found to contain two checks, one for The Kid and one for Ben Marcy—each for one thousand dollars. There was a short and to-the-point letter of commendation from the cattlemen's association, also.

"I reckon we'll have to go into the stock business on our own hook, Ben," grinned The Kid to Marcy.

"Well, the first thing I'm goin' to do is to go down an' see the girl in that store down to Dry Crossing that sold me some grub the night I first met you," declared Marcy. "She kidded me along in a way I like, an' I'm goin' to buy the biggest box of candy she's got in stock an' give it to her an' then stay an' help her eat it!"

Two days later The Kid and Lettie sat in the shade of the poplars.

"I'm sort of scared about Ben runnin' around," said the boy in a troubled voice. "That Musselshell sheriff is—" He checked himself with a guilty flush.

"I know all about it," said the girl gayly. "And Mr. Donald said he'd fix that business up all right."

"I always said Donald was a square shooter," said The Kid. "An' now, girlie, it's a nice day; the hills are lookin' good, an' we ain't got much to do 'cept talk, so I'm goin' to tell you the whole story."

She put her hand over his lips. "Let's talk about something else," she said softly.

"Why, I thought you wanted to hear all about everything!" exclaimed The Kid, looking surprised.

"I did," she replied, looking at him with sparkling eyes. "An' I didn't have to ask, for Mr. Donald told me all about it, an' he said you were 'quite a youngster.' I

115

called him down for that."

"He told you? You called him down?" The boy was astonished.

"Sure," she said saucily. "I told him you weren't a youngster. I said you were my *man!*"

A few minutes later she whispered from his shoulder.

"He said maybe I was right, an' if he needed another deputy over here he'd get the sheriff to appoint you."

"I don't think I could help him out," said The Kid happily. "I got my hands full now!"

CHAPTER XV
COPPERED TO WIN

Jerome was a town which had had its ups and downs for some thirty-odd years. Born overnight in the early days of the silver boom, it had weathered the depression in the price of that metal, had taken on new life when its hills disgorged stores of lead, had revived again when silver went up, and had achieved a permanent mild prosperity with the development of the big Jericho mine on the big hogback mountain southwest of it.

Such was its industrial chronology.

It held other attractions for those who were not interested in the hidden treasures of its hills. Isolated from the county seat by the high ridges and gleaming peaks of the Tenderfoot Range, it enjoyed a certain immunity from the law, despite the presence of Ed Mately, special deputy sheriff.

It was notorious for its resorts, where illicit liquor was sold openly, and where games of chance were conducted with the same freedom that prevailed in the banner days of the old West. This feature lured many picturesque and, in some cases, dubious characters—cow-punchers from the wide range lands of the Basin to eastward, prospectors and miners from the foothills and mountains, professional gamesters from towns throughout the north prairie country, rustlers who operated in the wild and tumbled bad lands to southward, fugitives who had lost their pursuers in the labyrinth of dim trails from the Canadian line to Wyoming's northern boundary.

With the burning of the mill the Jericho had shut down. The ore was not of a sufficiently high grade to ship out of the hills by truck, save in the form of concentrates. There had followed a month of inactivity. Miners left for other camps, where they were sure of work. Dark days loomed for Jerome.

Then had come the news that the Jericho would rebuild the mill. On the heels of this welcome information had come men to do the work. The company announced that it would rush construction, and Jerome awoke to the thrill of another boom. Truck drivers, carpenters, machinists, returning miners and muckers swarmed into the town, and its resorts, casting aside the proverbial lid, raised the limit to the sky and flourished.

The news that Jerome was booming and as wide-open as all outdoors filtered quickly through the mountains and spread over the far-reaching expanse of plain to east and north and south.

Finally it reached the alert ears of "Spider" Hawkins who was hibernating on the ranch of a friend in northern Wyoming. The Spider had thoughtfully remained concealed while the bearer of the message—a cow-puncher bound from the nearest town to a ranch farther south—had tarried for a space to pass the time of day and swap gossip with one of the ranch hands.

Spider Hawkins considered what he had heard with his customary composure. He was a taciturn man. It was only because of the glitter in his small, jet-black eyes that his friend could tell he was interested. If he could have read The Spider's thoughts he would have known that the small, wiry man, with the lean, tanned face and tight, cruel mouth, was exceedingly restive in his enforced seclusion. He would have known, too, as perhaps he did, that The Spider felt no remorse over his last shooting affair in which, with a jeering laugh upon his thin lips, he had sent a bullet into another man's heart.

The morning after he received the news, The Spider saddled his horse, a magnificent black, possessing exceptional powers of speed and endurance. A softened look came into the man's eyes, as he rubbed the animal's nose and spoke softly to him, calling him "Nighthawk." It wasn't a particularly savory name, and it was probably bestowed when The Spider had been in a facetious mood, for he had put in many lonesome hours as nighthawk with the last outfit he had worked with on the range; but, as he spoke it, a quality in his tone caused the big gelding to nuzzle him, shake his head and stamp, impatient to be off.

The Spider tied a light pack, wrapped in a black slicker, to the rear of his saddle, pulled on a pair of black leather chaps, tied down the end of the holster holding his gun, and swung into the saddle. He waved a farewell to the friend who had succored him during his temporary exile and struck north toward the mounting ridges which traced a series of great, green steps to the rock-bound ribs of a high divide.

For ten days The Spider traveled the mountain trails, avoiding the more generally used roads. He kept a ceaseless vigil while in the saddle and out, and he slept lightly. He smiled queerly and with evident relish, as the cool autumn wind hurdled the ridges and swept through the forests, stinging his face, and bringing the tang of ripened grasses, of pine and fir, and the elusive, faint aroma of the plains.

In the late afternoon of the tenth day following his departure from the Wyoming ranch, he looked down from the main pass over Tenderfoot Divide to where the town of Jerome showed like a brown smudge in its setting of cottonwoods, alders, and poplars. The landscape below the green of the pine timber was a flaming vista of variegated color. Vivid crimsons and saffrons spotted the foothill slopes, and far to the eastward the Basin lay in a golden haze, with pink and purple buttes marking its distances.

The Spider noted with keen interest the activity at the mine on the hogback mountain southwest of the town. Such activity meant a good pay roll, and healthy pay rolls were meat and drink to a booming, wide-open town.

He rode down from the pass with a grim smile of satisfaction playing on his lips and a gleam of anticipation in his eyes. Once again he was entering his natural environment, where a quick hand with card or gun turned the measure of advantage. The Spider was not one to let luck alone deal his game.

His horse attracted attention, as he rode along the short main street, but he paid no heed to curious glances directed at him. He rode leaning forward in the saddle, as though he were tired. But this was a habit of The Spider's; for under the brim of his black hat he saw everything and quickly took the measure of the town. He proceeded to the crowded stable in the rear of the Miners' Hotel.

"Don't know where I'll put him," said the stable man, looking at the newcomer's horse in undisguised admiration.

The Spider dismounted leisurely, eying the barn man with a frown.

"I was just going to tell you where to put him," he snapped.

The stableman looked up quickly, as he heard the voice. It was a voice which began in a drawl and ended like the crack of a whiplash.

"Put him in a stall," rasped The Spider.

He thrust a bill into the man's right palm.

"And see that he's well taken care of. Understand?"

It was the look in The Spider's eyes rather than the gratuity which impressed the stableman. He nodded with an attempt to grin. For some occult reason it did not seem proper to grin at this man. He hastened to carry out his orders. The Spider himself hung his saddle on a peg near the stall, which the stableman indicated.

"I expect to find that there when I want it, and I might want it most any time," he said.

The other inclined his head knowingly. "I'll keep an eye on it," he promised.

The Spider took his slicker pack into the hotel and succeeded in getting a room, despite the augmented demand for accommodations. He went upstairs to his room, stored his few belongings, locked the door, and descended to the street.

It was early evening, and the short thoroughfare was thronged with a motley crowd. The Spider appeared a diminutive figure among the big men from the hills and plains, and he looked particularly small now that he had discarded his chaps. He had a peculiar walk; he seemed to glide rather than to take deliberate steps. He sidled in and out of the crowd without apparent effort. His hat was pulled low over his eyes, yet his flashing glance missed nothing, and for an instant it hovered on the face of every man he passed.

As he made his way through the town, he noted the three resorts on his side of the street. The last of these, near the end of the street, flaunted a huge painted sign bearing the legend: "Plank's Place."

This was the largest resort in Jerome and The Spider entered it without hesitation. His small eyes glistened as he took in the scene with one comprehensive glance. Along the right was a long bar; to the left were card

121

tables, where stud poker was being dealt; to the rear, beyond the big, barrel stove, were other gaming tables, a roulette wheel, and a lunch counter.

Sidling through the crowd to the lunch counter, The Spider said: "Two cannibal sandwiches."

"What's that?" asked the puzzled man behind the counter.

"Two raw hamburger sandwiches," lisped The Spider; "and a side of Spokanes—that's beans."

The man in the spotted white apron scowled, but, as he caught the steady gleam of his customer's eyes, he turned to execute the order. Queer birds were drifting into Jerome these days.

Now The Spider's gaze roved over the place, as he ate. Finally it rested with interest on a table just behind the stove. There a white-haired man of stoic countenance and mien was dealing faro. The Spider tried to remember just how long it was since he had seen faro dealt; it had been years, he knew. When he had finished eating he paid his score and walked softly to the table bearing the faro layout. He glanced at the cases. Then from a pocket within his shirt he produced a worn, leather pocketbook and extracted a bank note. He laid it on the seven and kept the index finger of his left hand upon it until the dealer looked at him.

"Coppered to win," he said quietly.

The dealer raised his brows a small fraction of an inch, hesitated, then nodded silently. The Spider lifted his finger, while the other players stared at him and gazed in fascination at the bank note which he had wagered. It was a new, crisp, thousand-dollar bill.

CHAPTER XVI
A TENTATIVE DEAL

Dad Burkin, gambler of the old school which depended upon skill and knowledge of human nature rather than trickery, delayed his deal. He leaned over the box and looked down at The Spider.

"We'll have this all straight," he said quietly. "You're coppering the seven to lose next turn—it's the case card."

The Spider's face darkened. It may be that his explanation of his bet had purposely been a bit incongruous. The dealer's remark showed that he was shrewd and efficient and did not intend to leave any loophole for argument after the cards in the box had been turned.

"I'm coppering my bet, which means I'm playing the seven to lose," said The Spider with a sneer.

Burkin nodded gravely. He could read faces, and he already knew much about his aggressive patron. That the man had not chosen to use one of the disks provided for coppering bets he attributed to superstition. This seemed more likely because the man had made a large bet.

He resumed the deal. On the third turn the case seven lost. The dealer paid the thousand-dollar wager with ten one-hundred bills.

The Spider again glanced swiftly at the cases. He shifted to the right end of the layout and placed the two thousand dollars on the ace.

"Straight!" he snapped. "To win!"

"Can't let it ride," the dealer announced decisively. The Spider's head jerked back, and he met the dealer's eye with a narrow stare.

"Can't let it ride? Why not?"

"Too much," Burkin replied. "I've had a two-hundred-and-fifty-dollar limit. I let you bust it plenty once, and I stood as good a chance to lose as you did. I can't let you double it."

"You're a piker!" jeered The Spider.

The attention of most of the men in the place was centered on the pair.

"I'm banking this game myself, and my stake is limited," Burkin explained. "Plank and Duffy aren't behind this game. I pay a share of the winnings, if there's any, and take the risk. I've got to be prepared to pay all bets."

Burkin was telling the truth. The old gambler had long been prey to a yearning to deal faro bank again. When the town had opened up this last time he had arranged with Tom Plank, who owned the resort, and Joe Duffy, who had the gambling privileges, to deal bank. They had agreed for two reasons: First, because Burkin was popular; second, because they thought faro, the squarest of all gambling games, would soon break him and enable them to hire him to deal stud. Perhaps he would go broke so strong that he would have to appeal to them for a loan, in which event they planned to insist that he aid in certain shady methods which they favored to relieve players of their money. Dad Burkin was too square for the Jerome gambling combine.

Of all this, however, The Spider knew nothing. He only knew that his bet of two thousand dollars had been refused. It was one of his lucky nights. He felt it in his very bones. He had the hunch which is the barometer of fortune to the confirmed gamester.

"So you're running a tinhorn game," he said loudly. "Why don't you put up a sign? I step in with a thousand-dollar bet and find myself shut off as soon as I make a win. How far would you have let me go if I'd lost?"

Burkin remained cool despite the insult.

"You can bet a thousand," he said quietly. "If you'd lost I probably would have let you double to try and get even. I like big stakes as well as you do, my friend, but I've got to be sure I can pay 'em."

Burkin's right hand had slipped unnoticed into his right coat pocket. The Spider glared. Then he picked up his money and jammed it into a pocket. He rapped on the table with the knuckles of his right hand and spoke in a voice pregnant with contempt.

"You're running a sheep-herder's game! Maybe you thought that thousand was my stake. I'd give you a run for all you've got and can steal and borrow, if you were game. You ain't a gambler. You're a four-flusher!"

Burkin's lips tightened. But he was warned by instinct and intuition that here was a gunman—a genuine killer. Burkin knew the breed. He could almost see the hopeful menace radiating from the man who stood across the table from him. He tried in vain to place him; and, despite his resentment, he retained his caution.

"I happen to be the man that's running the game," he said coolly. "If you don't like the game I'll have to miss your play."

The Spider laughed in his face. The dealer had taken water. For the time being it was enough.

He slipped past the stove to the bar. The glances of nearly all in the room followed him. A tall, awkward-appearing cow-puncher, who evidently had been too free with the treacherous white liquor which was being served, took a step out from the bar and called:

"C'me on, little feller, an' have a snort. If you kin drink like you can talk you're some high-stepper."

The Spider whirled on him with a snarl of rage. He was highly sensitive about his small stature. In a move far too fast for the interested spectators to follow, he whipped out his gun. It whirled in a half turn, and he grasped it by the barrel and brought its heavy butt crashing against the offender's mouth. The gun spun again and dropped into its holster.

"That'll teach you to keep your fool mouth shut," said The Spider.

The man he had hit staggered back. Blood dripped from his bruised lips. Wonderingly he put a hand to his mouth and brought away two teeth which had been knocked out by The Spider's vicious blow. There was absolute silence in the place, as men stared at the darkened features of the wrathful Spider. They saw the man now was smiling; but the smile seemed a grimace of hate. They remembered his draw. Another gunman had found his way to Jerome. More than one man, who otherwise might have taken the part of either Burkin or the man who had been hit, remained silent and inactive before The Spider's darting glance. The presence of the little gunman seemed to fill the place.

Immediately two companions hastened to the aid of the befuddled puncher. Looking at The Spider coldly, they hurried his bleeding victim out of the rear door. The spectators took a long breath. The Spider stepped to the bar. He didn't voice his order, but tapped on the bar with a slim, brown, tapered forefinger and looked significantly at the man who was serving the refreshments. The bartender set out a bottle of white liquor and a glass. The Spider poured himself a generous drink and tossed it off in a gulp, without taking his eyes from the mirror behind the bar, in which he maintained his vigil on the others in the place.

He dropped a half dollar beside his empty glass and started for the front door. He had nearly reached it when he was intercepted by a large, florid man who smiled at him friendly.

"I'm Plank," said the large man. "I run this place, an' I'd like to have a word or two with you."

The Spider frowned and eyed the other suspiciously, but Plank indicated a door to a small office at the upper end of the bar and started for it. The Spider hesitated, then followed. When they were inside Plank closed a small door which opened into the space behind the bar. He turned upon The Spider and, disregarding the menacing glitter in the man's eyes, looked him over at length.

"Have a chair," he invited, seating himself at a rolltop desk and nodding toward a chair beside it. "And—

have a cigar." He proffered a box.

The Spider accepted the smoke and a light and sat down.

"What's the lay?" he asked, scowling. "Sore because I tried to get action at the bank, or because I rapped that fool meddler?"

"No," replied Plank with a short laugh; "I'd just as soon you'd have busted Burkin's bank. I don't want him dealing faro in here, but I've got to humor him, for he's one of the best men in the slot of a card table I ever saw, an' he works for me most of the time. I let him run that bank, thinking he'd break himself before this. He's been lucky, that's all. I'm not interested in your trouble with that other fellow."

"I'll break that tinhorn bank yet, if I can get a play out of him," said The Spider, clicking his teeth.

"Go to it, an' if you ain't got enough maybe I'll stake you," said Plank.

"So?" sneered The Spider. "You want to make out you're plumb liberal? I don't need any man to stake me. If I go broke I can sure stake myself—an' quick."

Plank looked at him speculatively. Thousand-dollar bills were not plentiful. Mostly they were in banks, or in express packages en route to banks. He did not for a minute doubt the ability of the small, dark man to rob either a bank, an express car, or a stage carrying express matter; nor was he particularly interested in that feature.

"You're a gunman," he said suddenly.

The remark took The Spider by surprise, and he showed it.

"I reckon you're the wisest man in this town," he jeered.

Plank leaned toward him. "I'm wise enough to know a gun fighter when I see him," he said evenly. "I can spot one as far as I can lamp him. But they ain't all good ones. You're a good one."

"You mean you saw me draw out there to crack that meddler?"

"I saw it," Plank agreed. "But you didn't hurry none. You can beat that draw when there's real shooting to be done."

The look in The Spider's eyes became coolly calculating. "How much conversation you going to sling around before you get down to what you want to say?" he asked.

"That's talk," said Plank, leaning back in his chair. "I own this place, and with Joe Duffy I practically control the games in this town. We're bothered now an' then by upstarts an' would-be gangsters, an' neither of us is especially handy with a gun. We need a man of your caliber. We're halfway protected, you might say, so far's the law is concerned. They don't bother us much. The county-seat bunch leaves us pretty much alone. We've a deputy here, but—well, it would be pretty hard for one man to put anything over here." He winked significantly. "We could strengthen our position some if we had a man like yourself on our pay roll," he concluded.

"I see," said The Spider. "You want to hire somebody to do your shooting. Now maybe you'll hint around as to just who you are gunning for."

Plank shifted uneasily in his chair. "I won't say we're out to get *any*body," he said. "It's just a—a safety-first proposition. We'll put it that way. Somebody might drop in an' start a heap of trouble, an' we want to be ready for him or them—that's all. Anyway, that's about all I know of to tell you right now."

"I see," said The Spider with a twisted smile. "I'm to get this in small doses. Maybe you think it would be too much for my delicate feelings to hear the whole story right off the bat. You want to fasten to the fact that I ain't advertised myself as no killer looking for a job."

"An' you want to remember that I don't know who you are—yet," returned Plank.

"Wanting references?" The Spider sneered. "Looks to me that you took a lot for sure and certain. I reckon you figure you can hire anybody you want, to do anything you want him to do. You start in pretty strong with a man who's a stranger to you."

"I told you why," said Plank tartly. "I spotted you for the goods, or you wouldn't be sitting in this office. All I want to do is have you meet my partner, Joe Duffy, an' then we can all talk it over together. If I've got you pegged right, the job would be just your color; an' it would pay well. More'n that, you're safe from such annoying things as posses an' the like here with us. Maybe that don't interest you none," he hastened to add, as he saw the other's dark look; "but I just thought I'd mention it."

"It's all right to mention it as long as it ain't a threat," said The Spider with a hissing intake of breath.

Plank laughed and smote his palm with his fist. "Maybe we'll get to understand each other yet," he grinned, rising. "Want a drink?"

"No," scowled The Spider, getting to his feet. "When'll this partner of yours be around?"

"He'll be in most any time; but you hadn't better wait around—unless you want to play. Maybe it would be wiser for us to stage our conference outside the place somewhere. You at the hotel?"

The Spider hesitated, eying Plank coldly. Then he nodded.

"Fair enough," said Plank in a satisfied tone. "The hotel folks are our people. Suppose you go down there, an' we'll drop around later. Joe lives there anyway. We'll be there before twelve."

They left the office, and The Spider went out of the front door, the cynosure of all eyes. Only Dad Burkin, the faro dealer, looked searchingly at Plank.

CHAPTER XVII
FROM THE HIGH HILLS

In a fragrant meadow in a wide valley west of Milestone Peak, highest of the mountains which formed the Tenderfoot Range, a youth and a girl were standing. The bright, early morning sun turned the girl's hair to gold, and she made a pretty picture, with the white walls of a cabin and a slope of living green behind her and the brown grass of the meadow, spotted here and there with the crimson of serviceberry bushes,

131

about her. Her lips were parted, and her hair was flying in the light wind. The youth, tall, slender, dark, gray-eyed, looked at her with glad eyes and a smile of wholesome appreciation.

"Lettie, if you get much prettier I won't ever dare to take you out of these hills," he said in a low voice.

"Oh, Charley, you mustn't talk compliments when you know I don't want you to go away," the girl pouted.

He took her hands. "I've just naturally got to go, Lettie," he said earnestly. "You know your father an' I are planning to go into cattle up here in the spring, an' I want to see the ranger down below Jerome an' put in our application for forest range next year. The sooner it's done the better. Then there's some things I want down to my cabin. I won't be gone long. Anyway there ain't a chance for me to miss a certain ceremony Christmas day, girlie."

The girl's cheeks bloomed the color of roses, and she glanced up at him shyly. Then her eyes again became troubled.

"It seems like every time you go away, Charley, something happens. First it was that trouble when you had to—to—shoot Spike Harmon. Then that Bloomquin came along and tried to run off the cattle and get you mixed up in it, and you—you had that trouble with him. It seems like trouble just comes racing to meet you every time you go across Milestone, Charley."

The youth laughed and put an arm about her.

"Maybe the troubles are over, sweetheart," he said

hopefully. "Anyway, I'm not goin' to let 'em get me mixed up any more. I'm goin' to leave my gun at the cabin when I go into Jerome, an' I won't get it, I reckon, till I start back over here. All I want there is to see the ranger down at the ranger station, say hello to Dad Burkin, an' invite him up here to the wedding, an' make sure the trail over Milestone is in shape to drive cattle on, although we'll probably have to do some work to it in the spring."

"You won't be gone long, Charley?" she asked anxiously, reaching her arms up about his neck.

"No longer'n I have to, girlie," he assured her.

There followed five minutes of parting.

"Hey! You people think you're actin' for the movin' pictures?"

An old man was calling to them from the doorway of the cabin.

"Run back an' tell your dad to mind his own business," said the boy to the girl, with a laugh.

She walked toward the cabin, while the youth turned to a beautiful, big gray horse behind him. He patted the horse on the neck, as he gathered up the reins.

"Ironsides, you're sure havin' an easy life of it," he crooned to the gray. "Good grass an' water an' a girl feedin' you sugar regular an' no ridin'. C'me on—let's go!"

The Spectacular Kid swung into the saddle, and the gray trotted across the meadow toward the trail up Tenderfoot Creek, which led to a little-known path over the north shoulder of Milestone Peak. The boy waved his hat to the two figures in the doorway of the cabin.

133

The horse tossed his head, champed at the bit, and in other ways showed that he was glad to be on the trail again with his young master on his back. Known far and wide in the mountain country as the fastest, noblest horse that had ever come into the locality, Ironsides had almost as great a reputation as his owner.

He reached the secret pass over Milestone and began the steep descent on the eastern slope toward Jerome. He noted the trail with new interest, for it was over this trail that he and old John Reynolds intended to drive their beef cattle down to the railroad in the Basin for shipment to market. Jerome, too, would provide them with a small market for prime beef when the Jericho mine resumed operations on the larger scale the company planned.

The Kid smiled contentedly. He had a modest capital, including money he had saved when working with outfits in the Basin and in the Smith River country to the southward, part of a legacy from his foster father, Fred Renault, and a thousand dollars he had received from the Basin Cattlemen's Association for breaking up Bloomquin's rustling gang that summer. Three years, with any kind of luck, should spell success, he reasoned.

Some two miles above Jerome he turned off on a trail leading to the left, and half an hour later he rode into a small clearing, where a comfortable cabin was situated. It was in this cabin that Charley French and Fred Renault had lived for several years, except for intervals when the boy worked on ranches, and when Renault visited mountain and prairie towns to match his skill with other followers of the green-topped tables.

He went inside and quickly made up a pack of personal belongings which he intended to take back with him to the Reynolds place on Tenderfoot Creek. This task completed, he opened a small, concealed trapdoor in the floor under one of the bunks, drew his ivory-handled gun from its holster, wrapped it in a cloth, and deposited it in the small hiding place under the floor. He replaced the trapdoor, hung his cartridge belt with its empty holster on a peg near the door, and left, locking the door after him. He rode down to Jerome by a dimly marked trail and reached the hotel in midafternoon.

Surprise at the appearance of the town showed in his face. Jerome was booming as he never had seen it boom before. While most of the men working on the mine buildings were engaged at their labors, the hotel lobby and streets were filled with floaters and adventurers of all types; and the idle miners, who were waiting for the mill to be completed before returning to work underground, were much in evidence.

The youth found he could not obtain a room at the hotel that day at least. This, however, did not bother him, as he knew Dad Burkin would be able to put him up in his cabin. Burkin had been an old friend of Renault's, and since Renault's death he had been one of the few real friends the boy possessed. As The Kid turned from the hotel desk, he met Ed Mately, deputy sheriff for that isolated section of the county, with headquarters in Jerome. Mately looked at him inquiringly.

"Kid, I'm sorry to see you here," he said, after they had exchanged greetings. "This is a mighty poor time for you to be in town."

"So?" grinned the youth. "Well, for the last few months it seemed that every time I drifted in was a poor time to light. It can't be much worse now, even if there are more people here."

Mately drew him aside. "Kid, you know the reputation you've got. No, don't flare up! I'm not rubbing it in; I know you ain't none proud of it. But there's another man in town who's greased lightning an' then some with his gun. And I guess he's looking for trouble."

The boy's face clouded. Then he smiled, as he patted his hips.

"I'm not packing any artillery, Mately, an' if I was, I wouldn't be lookin' for a chance to use it. I'm through with that stuff. You know I *had* to go with Harmon an' Bloomquin; there wasn't any way to get out of it an' stay alive. But I'm not one to go lookin' for a chance to show my speed. Sufferin' coyotes! I'm goin' into the cattle-raisin' business."

"Fine," said Mately. "I wish I was in some such game. I haven't got a chance to keep things straight here. Plank and Duffy have opened the town up wide an' brought in a bunch of boosters to make sure their games'll pay. They're running things with a high hand an' cleaning up regularly every pay day. An' they've done a lot of propaganda work until they've got the people that live here an' the men that's here to work, thinking that this town has a *right* to do just as it

136

pleases. That's the worst of it. If there was a murder here tonight, I don't know if I could raise a posse of a dozen men to go out after the killer."

"That's bad, Mately," the boy agreed. "Seems to me that Jerome would be better off if it paid more attention to regular business. The Jericho is goin' to open up in good shape, an' that'll more'n likely make the owners of some of these other properties around here wake up. I'd like to see the town tame down a little, for I'm goin' into business myself. Oh, I'm not against gambling. Renault was a gambler, an' Dad Burkin's a gambler; but, dog-gone it, there's square gamblin', an' there's the other kind. Plank an' Duffy might just as well be out with blackjacks an' guns, the way they're gettin' it."

"That's true," nodded Mately. "An' I ain't so sure they're not out with guns. This hombre I was mentioning to you arrived three days ago. He hangs aroun' the games an' seems to be lookin' on an' playing like he was more than just an ordinary or professional gambler. I'm thinking that he's been hired by Plank and Duffy, but I don't know just what for."

"What does he look like?"

"Short, wiry, black—crooked legs. They call him Spider. Hangs out in Plank's place most of the time. Listen, Kid, don't get mixed up in anything. I was a little tangled up in my opinion of you at first, but I've come to know you pretty well, an' I know you're so much better'n that crowd that you're too good even to have trouble with 'em."

"Don't worry," laughed the boy. "I've roped an' hog

137

tied that word trouble an' dragged it out of my dictionary. So long."

He left Mately in the hotel and went down the street to a short-order restaurant, where he ordered and ate a good meal. Then he drifted slowly in the direction of Plank's place. He had to see Burkin to arrange for his accommodations for that night, and he expected that the old gambler would be in the resort. Next day he would ride on down to the ranger station, he told himself. He entered the resort and looked quickly about for Burkin. He saw him at his faro table. Then he caught sight of another man at the table whom he knew instantly by Mately's description. It was The Spider, playing the bank.

As he approached, he heard the small, dark man direct a slurring remark at Burkin. His eyes narrowed, but he caught a warning look from the old gambler. He also heard whispers and guarded exclamations from the men at the bar and the card tables.

Then Plank's voice boomed out:

"Well, well, if The Spectacular Kid ain't come to town!"

CHAPTER XVIII
DUBIOUS ADVICE

The youth swung about on his heel, as he heard the hateful name called out. It was as The Spectacular Kid that he was known over such a wide territory as a gunman, and he was trying to live it down.

Now he turned on Plank, not so much because of resentment as because of surprise. Plank never had been familiar with him. He had hardly known the man. Why then should he take it upon himself to advertise his arrival so publicly? Even as he swung about, he noted two things: The Spider looked up so swiftly that his head bobbed like the dart of a rattlesnake; and in that instant a look flashed between The Spider and Plank, who was standing at the upper end of the bar.

"Hello, Kid! In to stay a while?" Plank held out a fat hand.

The boy ignored it. "What was the big idea, Plank?" he asked in a drawling voice. "Why all the shouted information?"

"Long time, no see," answered the resort proprietor, with a sweeping gesture of the hand which the youth had refused. "Thought maybe you'd been down South somewheres putting a few slow-handed gun toters out of the way. You're the boy that can put 'em under the daisies, Kid."

He smacked his lips and smirked with the air of one who is conveying a great compliment for the edification of any who might be listening.

"Plank, that's a roundabout way of sayin' something that isn't true," said The Kid angrily. "The only times I've had any trouble with gun toters, as you call 'em, was when there was no chance to get away from it. An' I wouldn't call 'em gun toters. I'd call 'em first-class crooks. That's what Harmon an' Bloomquin was, if you was meanin' them."

Plank flushed angrily. Then a chilly light came into his eyes.

"That's all right, Kid," he said in a patronizing tone; "but don't come around here aimin' to start any more trouble. We won't stand for it. The boys are getting a good play here an' are being treated fair an' square, an' we don't propose to have 'em imposed on none. We're glad to have you around; but don't start nothing."

The Kid stared in amazement. Gradually he comprehended the force of Plank's remarkable statement. There were many in the place who did not know him. Indeed, there were ten or twenty strangers to each regular resident of Jerome in town at that time. Plank had deliberately stepped out of his way to create a false impression of The Kid. Without saying so in so many words he had conveyed the idea that The Kid was a gun fighter constantly looking for trouble, and that that was the reason for his present visit to Jerome.

Flaming resentment shone in The Kid's eyes. There was scorn in his glance, too.

"Plank, I can read you like a book," he said in a low, even voice. "You spread your hole card face up all over the table in that little speech. But you're not goin' to put anything over—I'm telling you that!"

The others in the place had paid rapt attention. Those who knew The Kid had whispered to others, and Plank's talk had convinced the rest. Already there was excitement in the air. It is the time-honored tradition of the West that two gunmen cannot live in the same town. There is hardly room for two killers in one county. Yet here were The Spider, a known gun fighter with a formidable reputation, and The Spectacular Kid, whose name was a byword in that locality, in the same room!

Men looked at one another and drew long breaths. It was one of those situations in which almost anything could happen—a situation which held much for spectators, and which might hold death for one or the other of the principals.

A glance in the glass apprised The Kid of the fact that The Spider had cashed in his checks at the faro bank and was picking his way through the crowd of onlookers toward the upper end of the bar. The boy now knew that Plank's boisterous greeting had been meant for The Spider's ears. He knew that Plank had no use for him; he suspected that Plank had been implicated with the rustlers he had routed and jailed; but Plank had been well covered up, and his name had not been mentioned in connection with the deal.

Still, The Kid had good and sufficient reasons to believe that Plank hated him, and he surmised that the burly proprietor of the resort feared him. At best it was a detestable condition of affairs.

He could see Burkin trying to catch his eye in the mirror behind the bar, and he knew that the old gambler, his friend, was again endeavoring to convey a silent warning.

All of this had the effect of puzzling The Kid. Also it made him a prey to curiosity. He wanted to find out what was in the wind. But he was not unmindful of the tactful hints which had been conveyed by Ed Mately.

He turned to the bar at Plank's side and ordered a

lemonade. In the glass he watched the approach of The Spider. He noted the slight stoop of the man, his sidling gait, as he eased his way through the onlookers who were crowded about the card tables. He saw, too, that, while The Spider wore his hat low over his eyes, he missed nothing of what was going on, and he concluded that the man's ears were as sharp as his darting glance.

Another quality about The Spider impressed him. He could not have told in so many words just what this quality was. But he recognized in the small, dark man the telltale movements and characteristics of the seasoned and expert gun fighter. There was not the slightest doubt in his mind but that The Spider could draw and shoot with the best gunmen who ever had come into that country.

The Spider stopped in front of Plank. He indicated The Kid with a flip of his left thumb.

"Friend of yours?" he asked in an insolent tone.

"That's The Spectacular Kid," replied Plank with a trace of a sneering inflection in his voice. "Say, Kid, I guess this gent wants to meet you."

The Kid turned slowly and looked The Spider in the eyes, but he didn't speak.

The Spider glanced again at Plank. "Did you say something about somebody coming in here to start trouble?"

"Oh, no," said Plank blandly. "I was just tipping The Kid off, that's all. He's young, an' sometimes he gets boisterous, an' I was handing him a little advice to lay off the rough stuff."

Plank was grinning. But he was the only man in the resort who saw any humor in the situation. There was certainly no humor in either The Kid's or The Spider's eyes. When their glances clashed, they were hard and cold. Even Burkin, who was watching intently, found himself wondering if the rule of jealousy, which ordinarily prevailed among men who were accomplished in the use of their weapons, would hold in the case of The Kid. He knew, of course, that the youth never deliberately sought trouble, knew he was not proud of his notoriety and not inclined to add to his reputation. But in the case of The Spider, Burkin knew the rule would hold steadfast.

The Spider now turned his whole attention to The Kid. He looked him over coolly and spread his crooked legs far apart. When he spoke it was in a voice brimming with domineering insolence; and his question caused the spectators and even Plank himself to start.

"How old was you when you began toting a gun?"

The Kid drained his glass of lemonade and put the empty glass down upon the bar.

"I was old enough, Spider, to know when it was loaded," he replied in a drawl.

Burkin, who had ceased dealing bank, because his players all were watching the little drama, stepped out of line with the stove and slipped his right hand into his coat pocket. The Kid saw his movement out of the corner of his eye and smiled inwardly. He knew the old gambler always carried an old-fashioned, but efficient, derringer in that pocket.

To the spectators it was apparent that the question put

by The Spider and The Kid's answer were fraught with meaning, although they did not understand the nature of it. But Burkin knew the words conveyed a challenge.

The Spider's eyes had narrowed. "I reckon it must be loaded today, then," he sneered. "I see you've got sense enough not to pack it."

"If that's your particular idea of good sense, Spider, your own gun must be empty," said The Kid leisurely.

"That's for you to find out," The Spider retorted through his teeth. "Listen here, young fellow, don't pack a gun around this town!"

"Oh, I see," said The Kid, lifting his brows. "That makes it easier. I didn't just get who you was. You're the town guardeen, I take it. Who gave you the job—Plank and Duffy?"

This was putting it straight up to The Spider and the combine headed by Plank.

The Spider's face purpled with rage. There had been insult in The Kid's tone. There had been more than that. The Kid had shown a keen insight into affairs; he was smart. But the thing which affronted The Spider was the realization that The Kid was not taking water. He was almost on the point of slapping The Kid's face, but thought better of it. His eyes glittered, as he spoke truthfully:

"I ain't talking for the town or Plank or anybody else. I'm talking for myself. That's good enough for me. I'm telling you not to pack your artillery during your short stay here. You're just in on a visit," he concluded with a sneer. "Don't forget that."

"Well, now, I hadn't figured on stayin' very long, that's a fact," The Kid confessed.

Plank's loud laugh again put The Spider in a good humor. He laughed, too. But both men sobered instantly when The Kid joined them in their merriment. He sensed that The Spider was baiting him; he recognized the laugh as meaning that The Spider thought he had backed down. He grinned with the realization that The Spider did not know that was just what he had done. For The Kid wanted no trouble. Possibly the spectators thought the same as The Spider did. But whatever the opinion, the fact remained that The Kid was not armed.

Plank turned away and went into his private office.

The Spider stepped close to The Kid and spoke in a low voice.

"You're warned off!" he said. "This ain't a healthy range for doggies." He swung on his heel and slipped quickly out of the front door.

At the insult The Kid's face had gone white. The Spider had virtually called him a calf. A moment afterward he was glad The Spider had gone. The Kid knew in his heart that if he had remained he would have struck him. That would have meant trouble and lots of it. He walked slowly toward Dad Burkin. All eyes followed him. The others in the place had not caught The Spider's last words, but they had seen The Kid turn pale. Was he afraid of The Spider? They grinned at each other significantly, as they resumed their games. The Kid spoke softly to Burkin.

"Sure you can stay at my cabin," Burkin said quickly

in a voice which reached only the ears of The Kid. "There's plenty of room. You can put your horse up in the shed behind the cabin. Going up now?"

"In an hour or two," The Kid replied. "I'll be there when you drift in for supper, if you want to come up there to eat."

"I'll be up," Burkin promised.

The Kid made his way back to the hotel and went around to the corral in the rear where he had left his horse. He mounted and rode up a trail through the timber which reached to the edge of town.

It was half past six and already dark when Burkin arrived at his cabin on a slope just at the western end of the town. He found The Kid in the kitchen with a hot supper on the stove.

"Somebody else has arrived," said Burkin, hanging up his hat and facing The Kid.

"Who's here?" asked The Kid, busying himself at the stove.

"Curt Donald," Burkin answered.

The Kid whistled softly. Curt Donald was the under-sheriff, with headquarters at the county seat.

"Curt Donald?" he said wonderingly. "Dad, what do you reckon brings the undersheriff here?"

But Burkin evidently did not hear the question. He was staring at the youth's right thigh, where a worn holster was tied fast. The light gleamed on ivory above the black leather. The Kid was wearing his gun!

CHAPTER XIX
INVISIBLE WHEELS

Burkin refrained from commenting on the fact that The Kid was armed. He had heard The Spider's veiled threat contained in the warning to the youth not to wear a gun in Jerome. Was The Kid now armed because he wanted to force The Spider to a show-down? Did he wish to match his skill and speed against that of the small, dark man who was so obviously a dangerous opponent? He did not put the question to the boy.

During the meal Burkin explained the situation in detail. Plank and Duffy were resolved to keep Jerome open at all cost. They were garnering a fortune at crooked cards and by selling moonshine which Burkin thoroughly believed they made themselves.

"They figure that here it is, along the middle of October, and that the sheriff wouldn't think of doing anything about the way things are running here until after election, which is three weeks away," he told The Kid.

"You know, Kid, I ain't in favor of a closed town," the old gambler went on. "This is a sort of last stand for me. I ain't good for anything but cards, because I've been at it too long." His eyes glowed with reminiscence.

"I've seen big play in my day, Kid; and so did that foster daddy of yours, Fred Renault, for that matter. We

147

played in some big games. But we played square." He brought his fist down on the table with force. "Those were gambling days. Yes, this is my last stand. They're letting me deal bank down at Plank's, and I know why. They want me to go stone broke, because they think they can make me run a crooked game for them then. Well, if I go broke, it will be worth it to have dealt bank again. I've always wanted to deal bank again before I passed along. But they can't make me go crooked if I'm broke any more than they could when I had a stake. So I'm sliding along easy with 'em to keep my faro layout on the table."

"What about The Spider?" asked The Kid softly.

Burkin's expressionless face clouded. "Him? He's a gunman and a bad one. I can read the signs, and I saw him draw once a few days back to hit a fellow with his gun. He's the goods. I think Plank and Duffy have hired him to scare away anybody who might make trouble for 'em, and I think he's been told to get my game. Anyway, he's stuck to beat me and break me, and he's come mighty near doing it twice."

The Kid pursed his lips. "Dad, The Spider was baiting me along today. I don't figure that he was trying to scare me out. I pegged him for bein' sore because I wasn't heeled. There's more to that Spider business than we know anything about."

"You mean you think Plank and Duffy have told him to get you?" Burkin asked quickly.

"I couldn't say that exactly," replied The Kid with a frown. "But Plank did take pains to holler out the fact that I was in his joint. The Spider busted in right pronto. But the way the thing looked made me think I'd be a lot safer with my shootin' iron than without it. I hustled up to my cabin and got it. All I know for sure is that Plank and Duffy don't like me a-tall, a-tall."

"The Spider's got a wonderful horse," mused Burkin. "Next to yours it's the best horse I ever did see."

"When did he get in?"

"Three or four days ago. Started right in at my layout with a thousand-dollar bet. I made that the limit for him, and he hasn't had any use for me since. I wouldn't have let him bet the thousand, but it gave me a thrill just like the old days."

"He just drifted in by accident?" The Kid inquired.

"No man comes to Jerome by accident these days," replied Burkin. "But I don't believe Plank or Duffy sent for him. It was his speed in getting his gun out to hit a fellow that caught Plank's attention. They went into Plank's private office, and I guess they made some kind of a deal. I'd be careful, Kid."

The Kid nodded gravely. "I ain't out for trouble, Dad," he said soberly. "But I wouldn't let Plank or Duffy put anything over on me if I could help it. I believe that pair was the ones that tried to fasten the blame for the rustling around here on Fred Renault."

They were startled by a knock on the door. The. Kid's right hand dropped below the top of the table, as Burkin went to the door and opened it cautiously.

The old gambler stepped back and swung the door wide.

"We're raided," he said with a smile.

The Kid rose, as Curt Donald and Ed Mately entered.

"Thought I'd find you two together," Donald greeted.

The Kid held out his hand to the undersheriff. He liked Donald because he knew he was game, and because Donald had trusted him when appearances were very much against him.

"Guess somebody must have been lying to me, Kid," said the undersheriff with a smile. "They told me you was in, minus your artillery, but I'd hate to come at you a-shootin' now."

The Kid laughed, while Mately looked at him keenly.

"You ain't figuring on going after The Spider, are you, Kid?" Mately asked suddenly.

The boy shook his head. "Just had me guessin' pretty hard, that's all," he explained. "When I don't know what it's all about I feel more comfortable with a little weight on my right leg."

Burkin had brought chairs, and they sat down. Curt Donald eyed The Kid speculatively before speaking.

"Kid, I'm here on official business, and I want to put something up to you before I can know whether to tell you about it, or not."

He looked quizzically at Burkin. "I don't know whether to talk in front of you, or not, Dad," he said with a wink. "I hear you're dealing bank down at Plank's place. This is more or less official."

Burkin rose with a smile. "You gave me just the lead I was looking for," he confessed. "I've got to get back to the game. I can't trust the man who sits in for me when I'm away. But if there's anything you want to see me about, I'll be down in the place, and I close down about two in the morning—sometimes one. You know where to find me."

The undersheriff's fine black eyes shone humorously. "I may have to take you in for running too square a game," he grinned. "Dad, faro is an outrageous fair game for a time and town like this. You'd make more money with a wheel."

"How many men are there left in this county that can deal faro bank and deal it right?" asked Burkin, his eyes flashing.

"I get you," laughed Donald. "If I wasn't cluttered up with a badge I might play a few stacks with you myself."

They bandied some small talk before Burkin took his departure, and, as the door closed after him, Donald became serious again.

"Charley, I'm going to put a proposition to you," he said earnestly. "I'm not going to tell you altogether *why* I present this proposition, and I'm not going to ask you to explain any answer you may make to me. The sheriff's office needs a man in this neck of the woods who knows the mountain country—all of it. The sheriff's office needs a man who can ride, who has sense, and who can handle a gun with the best of them, if the occasion requires. The sheriff is ready to put you on the pay roll, at a hundred and fifty a month and expenses, as a deputy, if you want the job."

The Kid's eyes widened. Twice the law had been hunting him; now the law wanted him for an ally. He flushed, as he looked at Curt Donald's clear eyes and clean-cut countenance. There was no mistaking the nature of Donald's proposition. It was put straightforwardly in man-to-man fashion and in a business way. It was an honor. It was an honor, particularly coming from Curt Donald, who was an infallible judge of men.

"I don't want you to look at this thing in the wrong way, Kid," Donald continued. "Do you know what I mean?" And, as The Kid nodded, he said: "There isn't anything unfair about being an officer if you *are* an officer. We want to get as good men as we can. Mately can't handle the situation here, and I guess you know why. You would be a big help. You've got a hard name as a gunman, Kid. You can turn your skill into a worthwhile channel that'll do some good if you take this job."

The Kid saw Mately looking at him eagerly. But he shook his head.

"No, Donald, I can't take it. Renault used to say that there was only one kind of a man he'd help jail, an' that was a man who'd shoot another in the back. I ain't putting it so strong, but I can't take it. Anyway, I'm goin' into the cattle business."

Donald rose briskly and held out his hand. "That's all there is to it," he said, smiling. "I won't ask you any questions, Kid. And I hope you make a go of your venture."

Mately was opening the door. He looked disappointed.

"You two goin' already?" asked The Kid, rising. He took Curt Donald's hand.

"Yep. I've got to pay a visit to Plank's place," said the undersheriff.

After they had gone The Kid stood with an unseeing gaze riveted on the closed door.

Curt Donald, most intrepid of the sheriff's aides, in Jerome! And Jerome lined up solid behind Plank and Duffy against the law! And The Spider on guard!

What was it Renault, his teacher, had so often said? Then he remembered:

"Give *any* man credit if he's game!"

The Kid began to pace the floor restlessly.

CHAPTER XX
THE SHOWDOWN

Within ten minutes of Curt Donald's arrival at six o'clock all Jerome knew the undersheriff was in town. On the occasions of his previous visits his presence had been the signal for certain miraculously rapid changes in the nature of the activities in the various resorts. The serving of the white liquor had been temporarily suspended, and the card games had been changed from poker and other "regular" gambling pastimes to full-handed tables of solo and hearts and panguingui. But on this occasion only one change was made in the daily routine. The sale of the illicit liquor was discontinued until, as customers were informed with a knowing wink, "the law got out of town." Therefore, when Curt Donald entered Plank's place that evening, he found the gaming tables running full blast.

There was a momentary lull, as he stood near the front

door and surveyed the room. But the boosters sprinkled among the "come-ons," as the non-professional players were called in Jerome, evidently had received their orders, and they saw to it that the games continued. Donald, accompanied by Ed Mately, walked slowly the entire length of the room and back to the upper end. There he faced the bar.

"Where's Plank?" he asked the bartender.

The man nodded toward the proprietor's private office up front.

"Tell him to come out here," Donald ordered.

The bartender walked to the little door behind the bar at its upper end, opened it, thrust in his head, and a few moments afterward retraced his steps.

"He says to g'wan in," he said to Donald none too cordially.

"Tell him to come out here!" thundered Donald in a voice which carried to every corner of the place.

Before the bartender could reach the little door, Plank appeared through the other door leading into the room. He was followed by Joe Duffy, a short, squat man, with red, shifty eyes.

"Oh, hello, Donald," said Plank affably, holding out his hand. "How's election looking?"

Donald took the proffered hand for a moment and shook hands quickly with Duffy.

"Election looks all right," he said briskly. "What I want to know is this: Aren't you boys going a little strong?"

Plank lifted his brows. "Strong? In what way?"

Donald made a sweeping gesture toward the games.

"Oh, that," said Plank with a smile. "Before election. *You* know." He poked the undersheriff lightly in the ribs.

Donald frowned. "No, I can't say that I know," he said slowly. "But I *do* know one thing and that's that you're going a little *better* than strong. You're going the *limit!* They're talking about it all over the county— yes, all over the State. The chief don't like it."

"Well, just tell him that there's a lot of boys here working on the new mill up at the Jericho, an' a lot of miners waiting till they can get back to work, an' a lot of them has votes, an' they're just having a little fun till things gets shaped around again. An' that's the truth." Plank smiled and nodded with another wink.

"I'm not down here on a political errand, Plank," said Donald coolly. "I'm here at the chief's orders. You're going at this thing a little too heavy, and you've got to tone it down."

"Got to tone what down?" demanded Plank, his gaze hardening.

"This gambling," replied Donald sharply. "Those two roulette wheels—the one here and the one across the street—have got to go. I'm bringing the information straight to headquarters." He looked Plank directly in the eye.

"What's the kick on the wheels?" countered Plank.

"Same's the kick on the crap games," Donald retorted. "The dice must go. So must the blackjack. They're not played anywhere else in the county."

"You comparing Jerome to the rest of the county?" cried Plank angrily.

"It's *in* the county, isn't it?" shot Donald. "Other towns say, 'Everything goes in Jerome, so why shouldn't everything go here?' The day of playing this town as an outside proposition has passed, Plank. Jerome's getting to be too important. It has a future. It has to get down to normal. Anyway, it's the chief's orders, and I'm here to see that they're carried out. There are just three games that can be played here, and those are the old stand-bys. You know what they are."

Play at the various tables virtually had ceased, for Donald's statements had been heard, and even the boosters and other employees were for the moment nonplused. The few old-timers and Plank and Duffy themselves had never known the undersheriff to speak with such a note of genuine authority. They knew he meant what he said.

"If you bother us, it'll cost you every vote in this neck of the woods!" shrilled Duffy.

"And it'll gain us more than that many again in other parts of the county," snapped Donald. "It would help us to close you down tighter than a clamshell. If you want to play politics, we'll take a hand, and we'll deal the game into the bargain!"

"That's cold turkey, Donald, but it ain't good sense, an' you know it," said Plank, his face white. "You said you wasn't here to play politics."

"I'm not!" Donald interrupted. "I'm here to tell you what to do, and to see that you do it."

"That's another proposition," Plank answered sulkily. "You can't put this over on us without giving us notice."

"I don't have to give you any notice, Plank, but I will. I give you twenty-four hours' notice. At this time tomorrow night these games have got to go. That's the last word."

Several men had sidled up to the bar and had taken their stand near Plank and Duffy. Donald had not seen a man in the place answering The Spider's description, which had been given him by Mately. He noted the movement of the men, however, and stepped back a pace. Ed Mately, standing behind him, was visibly nervous. Plank looked at him with a sneer.

"What's the matter with your deputy down here? Ain't he been running things all right? He hasn't seen much to kick about."

"One man, and especially a man who isn't an out-and-out gunman, can't enforce the chief's orders here at present, Plank. Mately's been up against it in more ways than one, as you know even better than I do. And, understand, Mately hasn't told me anything or complained."

"But he isn't a gunman, eh?" Plank shouted. "Then I suppose you *are!* I suppose you want to pour lead into these boys because they want to enjoy themselves!"

There was a murmur of rising voices in the room—muttered remarks of a scornful and threatening nature that portended more direct utterances. So well had Plank done his work that the patrons of his establishment actually looked upon him in the light of their champion! The men near Plank moved closer to him. They had hard faces, protruding jaws, evil-looking eyes; and they were openly defiant.

"Plank, you are making capital out of a misleading situation you have brought about yourself," said Donald sternly. "You are deliberately creating a false impression. You cannot get away with violence!"

"But *you'd* try to get away with it," roared Plank. "You'd—" His words froze on his tongue. The muttering also ceased, and the place became extraordinarily still.

Donald was aware that some one had slipped in the front door and was standing beside him. His eyes narrowed and flashed dangerously. Had The Spider arrived? The undersheriff whirled on his heel and stepped backward in surprise.

The Kid was standing there, looking keenly at Plank, an amused smile of tolerance on his lips. He saw that Plank was staring incredulously at the ivory butt of The Kid's gun in the holster on his right hip.

"A frame-up!" croaked Plank in a rage. "Look, gents, The Kid's thrown in with the law! I might have known it—him coming in almost at the same time Curt Donald did."

He shook a trembling fist in The Kid's face.

"I had your number from the start, months ago—you dirty double-crosser!" he cried hoarsely. "What would Fred Renault think of you now? What would he think—tell us that?"

The Kid's face went white. Donald started to speak, but the youth interrupted him.

"What do you mean by that, Plank?" he asked sharply.

"What do I mean?" sneered the big man. "He wants

to know what I mean, men. I mean I know you for what you are—*you stool pigeon!*"

The Kid started back a step. A flashing glance in the mirror as there was a movement behind him, showed that two men had leaped upon chairs just under the two large hanging lamps. The bartender was moving swiftly toward the huge lamp above the bar. Then The Kid struck out, sending his right fist crashing against Plank's jaw. An instant after the blow landed, as Plank was crumpling against the bar, The Kid swung with his left, catching Duffy below his right ear, as he was reaching for his hip. Then came darkness.

The Kid leaped backward and stumbled into a man. He struck out blindly, felt his blow land, and plunged toward the dim light which filtered in through the front door, drawing his gun. He saw three others close to him, grasped his weapon by its barrel, and brought it smashing against one of the shadows. A string of curses came in a vicious voice.

"Watch that door!" Plank was roaring at the top of his voice.

There was a movement of many feet, tables were scraping on the floor, chairs were being overturned, showers of checks and silver added to the din.

"If you harm The Kid, Plank, you'll hang!" sounded Donald's ringing voice above the uproar.

Some one plucked at The Kid's sleeve, drawing him backward. Two other forms loomed close. Then came the flash of a gun, and the room rocked with the echo of the first shot.

"Outside!" came Donald's voice close at hand.

The Kid's heart leaped. The forms before him were undoubtedly Donald and Mately. Red fire streaked again in the darkness, and a bullet tore through the glass in the door.

"Don't shoot!" cried Plank's voice.

The Kid stepped aside, as the forms passed him. Seizing a table he threw it in front of him and followed with two chairs. He was in a shadow. A breath of air swept through the place, and he knew the door had been opened. There was a press of bodies—men in pursuit and others anxious to get out—against the makeshift barrier. The Kid leaped to the doorway, passed through. A man came through behind him. He whirled, and in the dim light he saw Dad Burkin with his derringer in his right hand.

"This way," Donald called to him from a short distance.

"I thought you were already out," said the undersheriff, as The Kid and Burkin reached him.

They hurried around to the rear of the place. Lights shone again within the resort. Burkin turned to the rear door, dropping his derringer into his right coat pocket.

"I'm going back in," he said quickly. "It wouldn't do for me to be missing just now. You understand. Beat it to my cabin, the three of you. They'll calm down now that it's over."

As he hurriedly entered the resort, the three others stole away in the darkness.

CHAPTER XXI
THE SUPREME WAGER

When they had cleared the vicinity of Plank's place, Donald called a halt. Standing in the shadow of the trees he looked queerly at Charley French in the faint light of the stars.

"Kid, you shouldn't have come in like that," he said with much feeling. "I believe I know why you did it, and it was a fine thing. It was a big thing, Kid; but it won't do you any good. And I don't want you to get into any mess on my account."

The Kid was smiling to himself.

"Give *any* man credit if he's game!" It was as if the words spoken by Fred Renault were ringing in his ears. And Curt Donald had faced Plank and his bullies and hired thugs in his own stronghold.

What might not have happened if Plank had not come to himself in time to order the shooting stopped?

The Kid knew, through the exciting days of his youth which had been spent in the cow camps and the wild cow towns, what could take place in a short space of time when men of untamed natures gave their raging passions full rein.

"I didn't expect anything like this was going to happen when I went in there, Donald," he explained. "I guess I was the cause of it, all right; but I couldn't stand that name Plank called me. There's a lot of difference between—well, between the job you offered me an' what Plank called me. An' that crack about Renault got my goat."

"But suppose The Spider had been there?" Donald suggested.

"There wasn't a chance of him bein' there," The Kid grinned. "The Spider's holed up, an' he'll stay holed up till you get out of town. Plank an' Duffy are too wise to let you see their gunman on the job, an' The Spider, I reckon, don't want to have any conversation with any undersheriffs. From what I saw of him I figure his face has been on enough reward posters to paper a hiproof barn. He'll stay out of sight till you leave."

"An' I've got to go out in the morning," said Donald in a troubled voice. "I've got some business down in the Basin that's got to be attended to tomorrow afternoon. It'll be two days before I can get back. An' I gave Plank twenty-four hours' notice!"

"That's all right," The Kid assured him. "Plank'll close up tomorrow night on the dot. An' he'll stay closed for just about twenty-four hours. He'll be running again full blast about the time you get back here on your way from the Basin after you finish your business."

"I expect that's right," Donald agreed. "Well, I'm going to explain to him in a way which won't give him a chance to misunderstand me, that he made a mistake when he called you what he did tonight, Kid. I have no stool pigeons working for me, and even if I had I wouldn't think of making you any proposition except the brand that I made to you tonight."

"Donald, I know that. You've always shot square

with me," said The Kid soberly. "An' now I'm goin' to tell you something. I didn't turn down your offer because I thought there was anything wrong with the job. You know what a hard reputation Renault had? Well, it would surprise you to know that he had a lot of respect for several deputies; and one sheriff was his friend. It wasn't that I'd mind being a deputy—an' if I was one, I'd try to be a good one—but I'm kinda fond of these hills. I like to ride around 'em, an' there's a whole lot of fine things I see in the hills that maybe nobody else sees. Just a sunset will keep me watching till dark. I'd hate to live up here an' have to be watching out all the time for something that was wrong. Maybe you fathom what I'm gettin' at."

Donald laughed softly. "Kid, you're no mystery to me," he said cheerfully; "but you've a habit of causing me worry."

"An' don't say anything to Plank until you get back," said The Kid. "Give him time to cool off an' see reason. Anyway I paid him for that remark he made to me. I'll bet he's rubbing his jaw yet. If he hadn't had a pillow of fat hangin' on it that smash would have broke my hand."

Ed Mately, who had remained silent, now touched Donald on the sleeve.

"That's the kind of a play I've been up against here," he said earnestly. "I haven't had the ghost of a chance to keep this town anywheres near decent. I could arrest Plank and Duffy, and I wouldn't get 'em half a mile out of town before I'd be stopped with a bullet in my back. When you asked me to send word if the reports you'd heard were true, I wrote you the truth. I ain't the man for the job here. I can't handle it as it should be handled, and, what's more, I know it and won't make no bones about it. I'm going to send in my resignation."

Donald smote his palm with his fist. "By the glory, I'm going to make this town safe for anybody!" he exclaimed. "But first I'm going to get some sleep," he added.

"There's plenty of room up at Burkin's cabin where I'm staying," said The Kid.

"No, I've got a room at the hotel, thanks to my badge, but I think I'll turn in at Mately's place. I don't want to go up with you, Kid, because they might find out we were up there, and it might make things all the worse."

"I'm going down to the ranger station in the morning," said The Kid. "I'll ride down that far with you."

"All right," said Donald, as they parted; "but you better meet me outside the lower end of town."

When Burkin reached the cabin shortly after midnight he looked questioningly at The Kid.

The boy shook his head. "No, I'm not working for Donald, if that's what's in your mind," he said. "But, Dad, if Donald gets into trouble I aim to help him if I can, just on—on principle. I like him."

"I didn't know," said Burkin a bit wearily. "Plank made some strong talk down at the place after it was all over tonight, and he gave me the bad eye. He intends to close tomorrow night according to orders, but I don't think he'll keep the lid on long. But one more day will finish my game. I'm through down there tomorrow night, and I'm through for good with Plank, if I can make it stick."

"Look here, Dad, don't make any changes on my account," said The Kid earnestly. "As you say, it's the only business you've got, an' as long as the games run you might as well be in it. A player gets a fair deal with you, an' that's more'n could be said of any of the other games in this town."

Burkin sat down and looked at The Kid wistfully.

"Looks like you was born to be a running mate to trouble," he observed. "But, boy, you sure hit Plank tonight. He's got a lump on his jaw as big as a billiard ball, and he's powerful mad. He'll get you if he can—and any way he can. You've got to watch out for Plank, Kid."

"Did he know you went out with me?" asked The Kid.

"Certainly not. If he had I'd have heard from it."

The Kid walked over and put a hand on the old gambler's shoulder. "Thanks for what you did tonight, Dad," he said simply. "I reckon you an' the folks over the hill are the best friends I've got."

Burkin rose. He drew the derringer from his pocket.

"Kid, in all my long experience I've never shot a man. I've carried this gun for years, and I'm a pretty good shot with it. Even now I keep in practice. But I've never had to use it. Yet today I had my hand in my pocket twice and had its nose trained on two different men. I've always believed in hunches, and I have a hunch that I'm going to have to use that little gun after all—and soon."

The boy laughed, although his eyes were serious. "All this excitement is getting on your nerves, Dad," he said in a soothing voice. "So far's I'm concerned it'll be over tomorrow. I'm goin' down to the ranger station in the morning to see about a grazing permit for next year, an' tomorrow night I'm goin' to hit back over Milestone. I figure from what you said that if you had to do any shooting it would be on my account. Well, I ain't goin' to give you a chance to shoot for me, Dad. An' don't forget that in a pinch I can shoot for myself."

Burkin didn't reply to this. He sat thinking, while The Kid made ready for bed.

When The Kid went to his room the old man took the lamp from the kitchen to his own quarters. There he carefully cleaned and oiled the derringer, without an expression on his stolid face.

In the morning Curt Donald and The Kid rode out of town. Plank saw to it that the whole town knew they had left together. His spies were everywhere; they had ascertained that The Kid stayed the night before at Burkin's cabin, and they saw him leave with the under-sheriff, although the pair met beyond the lower end of town.

Plank announced at noon that the games would shut down at eight o'clock that night. As a result of this announcement there was a great rush to the tables. Many of the men engaged on the Jericho construction work laid off for the afternoon when they heard the news. It was not known if the games would be started again, and Plank and Duffy allowed the report to be circulated that it was a final closing down of the lid.

As a result, the construction men plunged to the extent of their resources and endeavored to draw in advance upon their pay; miners dug into their slender savings; truck drivers engaged in hauling material to the mine left their trucks standing in the street while they played. By one o'clock Plank and Duffy and the lesser members of the gambling combine were reaping such a harvest as had never been known in Jerome, even in its palmiest days!

Plank knew that while he might break the camp that day, he could open again within forty-eight hours, if he so desired, and the men would find money somewhere with which to buy checks in an effort to recoup the losses they had sustained.

In a way Curt Donald's ultimatum was reacting to his benefit. The Spider appeared shortly before noon. If he was chagrined because he had not been present the night before when The Kid had appeared wearing his gun, he did not voice his annoyance. Early in the afternoon he began to play the bank. For three hours he toyed with bets scattered on the different combinations, seldom playing a card straight, which never totaled more than a hundred or a hundred and fifty dollars. Then he peeled a thousand-dollar bill from his big roll and, ignoring the yellow checks totaling more than that sum piled before him, played it straight on the seven to win. The Spider had a penchant for the seven, nine, and ace.

Dad Burkin accepted the bet coolly, with a slight inclination of his head. Indeed, as the gunman made his bet, a new fire came into the old gambler's eyes. He had resolved that this would be his last day of dealing bank in Plank's place; perhaps it would be the last time he would deal faro during his life! The old, fascinating lure of the game quickened his blood. The Spider was out to beat him, not merely because the gambling combine so wished, but because he, The Spider, had a personal dislike for him and was trying to show him up. Dad Burkin's ordinarily impassive features displayed the glimmer of a smile. His whole bearing sharpened.

The seven lost.

"Two thousand?" asked The Spider with a sneer.

"On the seven to win?" queried Burkin with a slight lift of his brows.

"On the case seven to win," snarled The Spider, as he put down two one-thousand-dollar bills.

Again the seven lost.

Four sevens now had shown during the deal, and a fourth of the cards in the pack remained in the dealer's box.

"Shuffle 'em up, and I'll bet you five thousand that the first seven turned wins!" exclaimed The Spider.

"There are other gentlemen in this game," said Burkin coolly. "They might object as they have bets down."

"Hang the other gentlemen, as you call 'em!" cried The Spider. "Shuffle 'em up!"

There was a hasty retrieving of bets on the board by the other players.

Dad Burkin looked calmly about. "Is a new deal agreeable to you gentlemen?" he asked politely.

This appeared to madden The Spider. "Deal the cards! Playing for time won't get you anything."

The other players nodded assent. Burkin took the remaining cards out of the box and shuffled the pack.

"I'll cut 'em," snapped The Spider.

Burkin immediately passed the deck over to him. The Spider first shuffled them again himself, then cut them. Burkin watched his every move. It would have been impossible for The Spider to "frame" the deck, and evidently the man knew it, for he made no attempt to do so. When Burkin again took up the cards he put the deck in the center of the layout.

"Any one else wish to cut?" he asked.

The Spider looked at the other players, red showing in his eyes. None availed himself of the privilege. The Spider now laid two thousand-dollar bills and other bills of lesser denomination, making three thousand dollars more, on the seven at the left end of the layout to win. Practically no other bets were made. The players recognized the struggle between The Spider and Burkin as a more or less personal affair which might have an unexpected outcome. They had no wish to be involved, or to sprinkle the board with comparatively inconsequential wagers in the face of the big money which was being played. Plank himself came to look on, and eager spectators crowded about the table. On the sixth turn of the cards the first seven showed as the loser. An exclamation of anger escaped from The Spider.

"That's a good box you've got," he said evilly.

"It is," said Burkin readily. "It's a good, straight box. There are plenty of men in these hills, Spider, that knew me for years before they ever suspected you were on earth, and none of them ever knew me to deal or play crooked cards. You're up against the luck!"

"Call it that!" snarled The Spider. "I'll bet you the chunk on the seven to win—an' this stack of canaries on the nine to win."

He dropped his roll on the seven and pushed the stacks of yellow checks, each worth twenty dollars, to the nine.

Burkin rapidly sized up the stacks of checks. "Two thousand one hundred and forty," he announced, spreading the seven odd checks beside the five stacks. "Is there more than twenty thousand in that roll, Spider?" He pointed to the bank notes piled on the seven.

"Less'n half that, thanks to your dealing," said The Spider savagely.

"You're getting a fair deal, Spider," replied Burkin with a cold, clear look in his eyes.

He began to turn the cards. The nine lost in the second turn, to the accompaniment of The Spider's denunciations. Three more turns and the seven showed on the wrong side.

The Spider stepped back. His face was white. The spectators drew a deep breath. The bank had won five times in succession, yet all knew that it had won fairly, for Dad Burkin had been careful to make it apparent that The Spider was getting an absolutely square deal.

Burkin's hand was steady as steel, as he raked in his winnings.

The Spider glanced at Plank, but Plank turned away. If Plank had had any thought of coming to The Spider's rescue with more money, that thought had fled, now that such a large amount was involved. It would require nearly twenty thousand dollars to put The Spider even, and that much more might have to be risked in an effort to break Burkin.

The Spider's eyes filled with rage, as he noted Plank's indifference. He looked quickly at the cases. Two aces had shown, and both had won. His eyes gleamed, as he looked at Burkin.

"Know my horse?" he asked in a low voice.

Burkin nodded. "A fine animal," he said.

"I wouldn't take ten thousand for him if anybody wanted to buy him," said The Spider through his teeth. "I'll bet you my horse against five thousand that the next ace loses!"

There was a stir about the table. Every one sensed that in wagering his horse—one of the finest that had ever been seen in the mountain country—The Spider was wagering something which meant far more to him than five thousand dollars in cash. But, if he won, he would have a chance to play again and might retrieve his fortunes.

Burkin did not answer at once. He was not hesitating because he knew the horse was not worth five thousand dollars, save in a sentimental reckoning. If he refused he was nearly twenty thousand dollars winner. He had The Spider broke so far as cash was concerned.

It was fully within his rights to decline to accept the wager, or to put a fair valuation on the horse. In placing a valuation of five thousand dollars on the animal, The Spider was taking advantage of him because he was a heavy loser. Burkin did not like the idea of being "played," and he didn't want the horse. But if he deliberately gave The Spider a chance to get even in this way, the latter, if he lost, could hardly expect to gain an audience for any grievance arising out of the game. It was doubtless this last reflection which caused him to accept the wager.

"Your horse isn't worth five thousand, Spider," he said in a low voice; "and I have no use for him. But I'll give you a chance to get even. This time there's a big advantage on your side. The cases show two aces out, and both have won. The chances are two to one, anyway, I'd say, that the next ace loses."

"Trying to crawl out of it?" asked The Spider with a sneer.

"When I make a statement I stand by it," said Burkin in a louder tone. "This isn't hardly a time for you to be casting any reflections, Spider. Your horse isn't worth more than five hundred, but I'm putting up five thousand against him. You're coppering the ace?"

"You said it," barked The Spider. "I guess you'll have use for the horse all right, if you get him."

The spectators held their breath in excitement, as Burkin began to turn the cards. The Spider leaned low over the table, his eyes fixed on Burkin's slim, white, tapered fingers and the faces of the cards he disclosed one at a time. Play was all but suspended at the other tables. Plank was again looking on.

Two turns—three turns—four. On the fifth turn the ace of spades was revealed—*a winner!*

The Spider jumped back. "That ace of spades is as black as my horse an' your heart!" he shouted. "You can't tell me six wins for the bank would come up natural!"

"I've seen more straight wins than that," observed Burkin, as he shuffled the bills into his pockets.

"Then you was dealing an' somebody else was betting against 'em!" cried The Spider.

Burkin's face turned a shade paler. "These men were watching the deal the same as you, Spider," he said sharply. "They all know it was fair and square."

"Sure," sneered The Spider. "Bound to be with your wanting that black horse of mine to give to your stool-pigeon friend!"

"That's a bit strong, Spider," said Burkin, his eyes narrowing.

"Strong? Why wouldn't it be strong? Ain't you that dirty stool pigeon's running mate? Didn't he stay up at your place last night? Didn't he leave town with that undersheriff? Ain't he your particular friend?"

"The Kid is my friend," said Burkin stoutly, "and he's not a stool pigeon."

"No, he ain't!" shot The Spider through his teeth. "What'd he back up the undersheriff for last night? Good thing for him *I* wasn't here! An' you hobnobbing with him an' with the undersheriff too, probably, an' then coming down here an' running a game! You're a stool pigeon, too, you tinhorn! You're playing safe, an'

Plank an' Duffy are too blind to see it!"

Burkin's face was white as chalk. His hand had slipped into his right coat pocket, while The Spider was spitting out his words as fast as he could talk.

"Spider, if you say The Kid or me are stool pigeons, you lie, and your tongue is blacker than that ace of spades that was against you!" he said in a voice that rang through the room.

The Spider's lips froze to thin, white lines against his teeth. His beady, black eyes were pin points of angry flame. His muscles tensed, as he leaned a bit forward.

"I think you both are just that," he said in a hoarse whisper. "Draw, you double-crosser—draw!"

Burkin's hand jerked out of his pocket, just as a gun roared in the limited confines of the room. The old gambler's fingers relaxed, and the derringer fell upon the layout on the table. He leaned for a moment upon his check rack, staring at a curl of smoke rising from The Spider's right hip. Then he fell across the table.

The Spider backed quickly through the crowd, menacing the stupefied onlookers with his smoking gun, and a few moments later the rear door slammed after him.

CHAPTER XXII
THE WHITE VEIL

An hour after the shooting of Dad Burkin, while the hills still were bathed in the hazy afterglow of the sunset, filtering through a screen of scuttling clouds,

The Kid rode into Jerome from the road to the Basin. He had finished his business at the ranger station, where Curt Donald had taken leave of him, and he had immediately started on the back trail. Certain signs in the north skies had not been misinterpreted by the youth, who was familiar with the moods of the elements in the north-range country. There was a freshened wind, too, and a cold, dull luster to the film of cloud which mounted above the northern horizon.

As he entered the town, The Kid saw he was indeed an object of interest. He assumed that the events of the night before had added much to his reputation, and he smiled to himself, as he reflected that those who were eagerly anticipating more trouble would be disappointed. The Kid planned to visit Burkin's cabin, leave a note, if the old gambler should be absent, go directly to his own cabin above Jerome for his belongings, and then ride over Milestone to the Reynolds place.

This plan was forgotten two minutes after he began the ascent of the short trail from the western end of the town's street to the abode of Dad Burkin. He was met outside the door by Ed Mately. The deputy was nervous and excited, although his face was grave. The Kid wrinkled his brows in perplexity as he dismounted before Mately.

"What's up?" he asked, seeing that Mately made two unsuccessful efforts to speak.

"The Spider shot Dad Burkin!" Mately finally blurted.

The Kid's jaw dropped, then snapped shut with a click. He dropped his reins.

"Is he—dead?" he asked quickly.

Mately shook his head. "The doctor from the mines is in there."

The Kid waited to hear no more, but hurried to the cabin door, opened it, and slipped softly inside. A white-haired man, whom The Kid recognized as one of the employees at Plank's place, met him in the kitchen, putting a finger to his lips for silence.

"Where is he?" whispered The Kid, although he well knew that the wounded man must be in his bedroom.

At this juncture the Jericho mine's doctor, a friend of both Burkin and The Kid, came noiselessly into the kitchen with some pieces of soiled bandage and absorbent cotton in his hands. The boy's face went white, as he saw the crimson stains. He looked questioningly at the doctor. The physician gave the bandage and cotton to the other man with whispered instructions and nodded to The Kid to step outside. In the little plot of grass before the cabin he answered the interrogation in The Kid's eyes.

"Hit above the heart to the left," he said gravely. "Bullet clipped off a tip of the shoulder blade behind."

"Will he live?" asked The Kid in a low, tremulous voice.

"He might."

But The Kid could tell by the way the doctor spoke that he didn't think Burkin had a chance to recover.

"He's unconscious," the doctor said. "You can see him, but that's all."

The Kid went in with the doctor and looked down upon the white face of his friend. The wounded man

176

was hardly breathing. In that moment a deep rage was born in the boy's heart against the boasting killer who had shot Burkin down. He had not heard the story, but he knew, as well as if he had been present, that the shooting had not been brought about by the old gambler—that whatever Burkin had done to enrage The Spider had been actuated by Burkin's faithful devotion to his principles. And Burkin had been his and Fred Renault's one friend in the untamed town of Jerome. He beckoned to the doctor to follow him, and again he stepped outside.

"Stay with him and do everything you can," he told the doctor. "I'll have friends here to nurse him and look after him before—well, by midnight, if I can; but by early morning, anyway."

The doctor nodded, as The Kid leaped into his saddle and sent the big gray plunging down the trail. The boy rode straight to the barn in the rear of the hotel. Then he hurled a question at the stableman in a voice which brought an immediate answer.

"Took his horse outa here more'n an hour ago," said the man. "Seemed in a powerful hurry; didn't take time to pay what he owed."

But The Kid was riding away.

On the road west of town he overtook Ed Mately and rode with the deputy for two miles. Mately quickly gave him the facts about the shooting, as he had managed to learn them from spectators. The Kid muttered under his breath. His face was still white; his lips pressed firmly together.

"I'm hitting for the main pass," Mately told him.

177

"What did I tell you about raising a posse to chase a killer if I had to? I couldn't get a man to go with me to chase The Spider. I knew you'd be along; but I didn't think you'd want to leave Burkin so quick."

"I'm goin' after a nurse," said the boy.

"Not—not over the Milestone pass on a night like this promises to be!" gasped Mately.

"Yes," flashed The Kid. "I couldn't do it on any other horse."

It was dark when The Kid left Mately and turned his horse up a steep, narrow trail which wound through the thick timber up and up—ever at a steep grade—toward the north shoulder of Milestone Peak. Clouds were flying overhead, and a cold wind tore down from the Divide, screeching through the timber and whipping branches into The Kid's face. Encouraged by the voice of his master, the big gray made splendid headway, following unerringly the trail he had traversed so many times before.

All of the sky to northward was a mass of clouds, riding on a high wind, mounting steadily into the high arch overhead, obscuring the light of the stars. By midnight it would be black as pitch; but The Kid, instead of looking apprehensive, smiled grimly at the thought.

The Spider had more than likely struck out for the hills. If he had left by the road to the Basin, The Kid would have seen him. Then, too, he would fast get into civilization in that direction, and The Kid believed a man of the stamp The Spider indubitably was, would wish to avoid a thickly populated district, such as the

178

Basin had come to be with the dawning era of agriculture.

If he had taken the trail to the main pass over the Divide above the Jericho, he would come to a branch in the trail when he had crossed the backbone of the mountains. One branch led south toward Smith River, the other led northwest into the mountains—up the Tenderfoot to Starvation Ridge and the Blizzard Flats. The trails in either direction would be hard to follow on an inky night by a rider who was not thoroughly familiar with the country.

Thus, while The Spider had miles and miles of virtually uncharted wilderness in which to make good his escape, the very wild nature of the territory he had entered might trap him! Two hours after he left Mately, The Kid was over the secret pass on the north shoulder of Milestone. He made far better time on the western slope, which was not as steep as the eastern side, and in another hour had reached the falls of Tenderfoot Creek. He swung down the creek at a gallop and soon dashed into the meadow, where a light proclaimed the location of the Reynolds cabin.

John Reynolds and the girl, Lettie, welcomed him joyously, but sobered quickly, as they noted his grave look. In as few words as possible he told them what had happened in Jerome. Before he had finished, Lettie left them, and they heard her making hurried preparations in her room. John Reynolds looked at the clock on a shelf in the kitchen, as The Kid's voice died.

"Lucky I brought the horses up to the south pasture today," he said. "An' my horse is in the barn. Looked like we might get a little weather."

They were silent for a spell. Dad Burkin had been a friend of John Reynolds. Presently the girl appeared with a small bundle.

"You going to take us down tonight, Charley?" she asked.

"No," said The Kid. "I'm going to let you ride my gray, Ironsides, an he'll take you down."

John Reynolds looked at him quickly.

"She'll be safe on Ironsides," The Kid explained; "an' the big gray knows that trail as well as I do—better on a dark night."

"You're going to stay here?" asked John Reynolds.

"Till morning," replied the boy. "I'll pick out the best horse in the pasture an' take a look around."

"You think The Spider maybe came this way?" Reynolds asked after a time.

The Kid nodded gravely, while the girl gazed at him anxiously.

"I told Mately to go south, as long as I was comin' up here," he explained. "I expect you better get down there to look after Dad as soon as you can. Let the gray have his head, Lettie, an' he'll take you there as fast as he can, soon's he knows where he's headed for."

The girl smiled at him bravely. Shortly afterward he pressed her hand tenderly, as she sat in his saddle on the big gray. It was nearly pitch dark, as the girl and her father started up the trail to the pass on Milestone. The Kid turned back to the cabin. It was near midnight.

By sending the girl on his gray horse he was certain that she and her father would reach Jerome in a few hours—certainly before dawn. The gray knew the trail and would lead Reynolds' horse. Meanwhile The Kid was getting the advantage of several hours in the matter of taking up the chase for The Spider. If he had ridden the gray to Jerome to guide Reynolds and the girl, he would have had to get a fresh horse before he could take up The Spider's trail. That would mean several precious hours and a fagged mount before he arrived back on the Tenderfoot.

As it was, if The Spider had come that way he would have to camp for the night, and The Kid would have an excellent chance of catching up with him in the morning, regardless of the fact that he would have to ride a slower horse. For The Spider could not hope to follow the dim trails north of the Tenderfoot on such a dark night, being, as The Kid believed he was, unfamiliar with the locality.

The Kid extinguished the lamp and stretched himself out upon a couch in the little living room. He seemed scarcely to close his eyes and open them when he detected the faint glimmer of the dawn through the window curtains. The cabin shook in the force of the wind.

He quickly built a fire and put coffee on to boil. Then he took his rope, which he had retained, walked briskly the length of the meadow through a clump of young firs to the pasture John Reynolds had spoken of the night before. There were several horses in the fenced inclosure, and the boy selected a bay which he had ridden before, and which, indeed, had been in Renault's string and had thus become his own property. He roped the horse and rode him, despite his pitching, back to the cabin. There he put on an extra saddle and bridle which also had once been Renault's property. Except from the standpoint of speed, The Kid now had a good, strong horse and a saddle to which he was accustomed. He drank the coffee and ate some bread and cold meat which he found in a cupboard. It was not yet broad day when he rode down to the Tenderfoot trail and started up the creek.

He had no way of knowing if The Spider had come in that direction or, if he had so come, how far he had got; but he knew he would have an excellent view of the country for miles when he reached the western end of Starvation Ridge at the head of the creek and so could detect The Spider's presence in the vicinity.

The sky was cold and lowering, and a biting wind was bearing down from the north. It was the season which is the dividing period between fall and winter in the mountain country, when the first real storm out of the north brings the snow which lies upon the ridges until spring. The Kid had not gone fifty yards up the trail which forked above the falls, when he reined in his mount with a smothered exclamation. There were fresh tracks in the trail. A horse had passed that way a short time before, or during the early morning hours after midnight!

Quickly the youth estimated the time it would require for The Spider to reach that spot by way of the main pass. If he had traveled steadily at a moderate pace he could have been there at least an hour before dawn. The Spider, if it indeed were he, was a better man on the trail than The Kid had suspected.

The boy used his steel and rode rapidly ahead. At the western end of Starvation Ridge his heart gave a bound. There were two trails here; one led westward in the direction of the county seat; the other led northeastward along the crest of the ridge. This last was a poor trail which came out on Blizzard Flats, miles from anywhere and almost directly north of the site of Jerome. The rider who had passed that way had taken this last trail.

Now The Kid galloped along the ridge. He had not reached its end when he saw a rider on the long, shale slope leading down to the flats.

He swerved his mount and edged down the farther side of the crest of the ridge. Then he drove in his spurs and raced in the direction of the shale slope, concealed from the rider ahead. When he had nearly reached the end of the ridge he again swung up in full view on its crest. As he had expected, he found he was at the top of the slope. The rider ahead had all but reached the edge of the flats.

Even at that considerable distance The Kid recognized The Spider on his famous black horse. But that horse, as The Kid well knew, was fagged. He had been ridden all night on a strange trail. The boy turned his mount down the slope and with utter disregard for the danger plunged and slid in the soft shale, sending up a cloud of dust to ride on the wind. Then The Kid saw something else which caused his pulse to quicken. Far away across the flats on the northeastern horizon there was a white film. Even as he looked, it mounted higher against the gray sky; became more distinct. It bore the appearance of a thick mist or fog, drifting across the land—a great, white veil, which the wind was bringing in its train.

But The Kid knew the meaning of the unusual sight. The white veil was the first blizzard of the winter sweeping down from the north. The Spider had gained the flats and had seen him. The big black plunged ahead in a heartbreaking burst of speed which taxed every ounce of his strength and endurance. The Kid's horse came out of the shale onto the solid footing on the far-reaching plateau. Then both riders, one in frenzied flight and the other in relentless pursuit, dashed toward the icy mist racing across the land.

CHAPTER XXIII
IN THE STORM

That the race would be of short duration soon became apparent to The Kid, who was pushing the bay at his top speed. The Spider began to slacken his pace when only a comparatively short distance out on the plateau. Although The Kid surmised that his quarry's big black was far from fresh and not good for a long run at great speed, the sudden checking of The Spider's pace made him wary. He took only partial advantage of the opportunity thus afforded to close up the gap between them.

Meanwhile the blizzard came on at terrific speed— speed which was confusing because of the ease with

184

which the swirling snow was carried by the wind, and its gradual approach, as seen by the eye. Yet The Kid knew that The Spider, evidently an old-timer in the north-range country, must be aware of this deceiving feature of the onrushing storm. The blizzard would be upon them with disconcerting suddenness.

The Kid urged his mount to a faster pace. This had the effect of causing The Spider to swing off to the east. As The Kid followed him, they were no longer riding directly into the teeth of the storm. Then The Spider suddenly raised his right arm, leaned to the left, and sent a bullet whistling in The Kid's direction. The boy laughed mirthlessly. The distance was too great, and the target too uncertain for anything but a chance shot to hit him. If The Spider expected that this move would check the pursuit he was disappointed. He shot twice again without result, and then The Kid became aware of the gunman's purpose.

The Spider, with quick glances north across the flats, suddenly increased his pace, driving in his spurs cruelly and sending the big black into a great burst of speed, shooting back over his shoulder, as he did so, evidently in the hope that some of his shots would chance to find their mark.

Looking northward The Kid saw that the veil of snow was almost upon them. The Spider's ruse was disclosed. He intended to dash into the teeth of the storm and lose his pursuer in the blinding snow which the wind was hurling with wild ferocity across the flats. It would be impossible to see more than a few yards, or rods at most, in the storm; and The Spider planned to let the swirling snow cover up his escape.

The Spider now, with a better lead, whirled his horse directly north and raked him with his spurs. But The Kid already had cut to the north and was also racing toward the white storm curtain. Then the blizzard was upon them.

As soon as the storm hit him, The Kid again turned his horse east. He could dimly see the wavering figure of horse and rider ahead of him. Then in a gust of wind and snow he lost sight of the forms ahead. But he did not change his course. A minute later, when it was almost too late, he divined the real purpose which had been behind The Spider's surprising move. From near at hand to the left of him came a veritable volley of shots! The Spider had circled around him—had deliberately planned an ambush under cover of the storm.

The Kid whirled his horse, but was unable to see The Spider, who had evidently ridden on or had had trouble with his mount in the blinding sting of the snow-filled wind. Anyway, the man had disappeared. The boy was boiling with scornful anger. If The Spider wanted to shoot it out, why didn't he meet the man he sought to kill in a fair gun play? Had not The Spider openly exhibited and boasted of his draw? Had the things he had heard of The Kid made him doubtful of the result if the two should meet? Did he seek to take an unfair advantage because he was afraid of the outcome?

Such reflections caused the boy to feel an ungovernable contempt for the man, whose shooting of Burkin was nothing short of premeditated murder—it would virtually be that if Burkin should die. Perhaps the old gambler was already dead!

The thought stung The Kid to action. He dashed in a wide circle in an effort to sight the man on the black horse. This failing, he circled again, scanning the snow-covered ground as best he could. He was rewarded by sight of tracks, and, leaning over the neck of his horse, he saw that the tracks led southward. The Spider was running with the storm.

As The Kid sent the bay again flying in pursuit, he realized that this was the result of clever reasoning on The Spider's part. The man must know that it would be folly to head north across the flats to the far-reaching open prairie country. There it would be but a question of time before he would become lost.

To the southward, however, he would come to the timber on the slopes which led down from the flats and Starvation Ridge to the hills north of Jerome, below Milestone Peak. In the timber there would be respite from the full force of the blizzard. But, also, there would be but one way out, unless The Spider should again decide to brave the fury of the storm and head north; and that one way out was through Jerome. There was another way, as The Kid knew; but it was by dim trails leading around the eastern end of Starvation and across several ridges to the secret trail over Milestone Peak, of which The Kid did not believe The Spider knew. On the flats they were slightly east of Milestone, having crossed the Divide again by way of Starvation Ridge.

Now, as The Kid spurred his horse southward, he

found that The Spider was leaving a trail which was becoming more and more plain—it was as if the fugitive were writing the story of his flight on the flats. For the snow, falling on the ground, which still retained considerable warmth, melted to an extent and wet the soil, and the soil of the flats was gumbo, that fearsome mud which bakes hard and cracks in the sun and becomes as slippery as ice and as clinging as glue when wet.

The flying hoofs of The Spider's mount caught up patches of the softened mud and flung them behind, leaving a trail which The Kid experienced no difficulty in following, for the dark splotches showed vividly against the white underneath. The Kid's own horse began to slip and slide in the mud, and he had to check his fast pace. But he was satisfied that The Spider's progress also was being impeded in the same way.

For two hours he rode steadily on The Spider's trail. He knew they had passed the east end of Starvation above them on the right. Finally he caught sight of a shadow ahead and realized that he was approaching the upper edge of the timbered slopes.

With this knowledge he left the plainly marked trail and swung to the west. It was quite possible that The Spider would rest his horse when he reached the timber; it was also more than likely that he would keep a sharp lookout for a time from the shelter of the trees to ascertain if he was being followed. This probable vigil on the part of the man he was after did not interest The Kid, except that it might give The Spider a feeling of security if he did not catch a glimpse of his pursuer;

also a feeling of such security would doubtless result in The Spider's making a move which would give away his plan.

The Kid rode some distance west, then continued on to the edge of the timber. His movements now became more and more cautious. He followed the line of pines just below the edge of the plateau until he was convinced that he was near the spot where The Spider had entered the timber, if he had entered it. Here he dismounted and rested his horse, while he scanned the line of trees as far as he could see in the storm.

For some time he remained attentive, and then he mounted again, and slowly picked his way along the timber. After a few minutes he left the saddle again and led his horse in among the trees. He tied the bay and proceeded on foot, picking his way carefully as he had done many times when stalking game in the mountains.

In this way he came upon the tracks left by The Spider's horse. They were plainly marked on a narrow trail leading down the slope from the edge of the plateau. The Spider evidently had followed along the timber until he had come to this trail. The Kid smiled with grim satisfaction. It now was apparent that The Spider intentionally, or without knowing it, was headed back toward Jerome.

The boy retraced his steps to where he had left his horse. He then led the animal out of the timber and rode along the edge till he came to the place where The Spider had noticed the trail. He saw that The Spider had come up along the timber for a short distance, and that he had waited at the opening to the trail for a short time, as the tracks showed he had dismounted there and moved about on foot.

It was apparent that The Spider had assumed, and rightly, that the trail would lead to other trails and in time converge with a road leading to some habitation, as was usual with the paths in the hills; but The Kid doubted if The Spider knew he had gone around Milestone Peak and was headed back in the direction from which he had come.

The Kid did not hesitate to strike out on the trail. The force of the blizzard's blast was broken by the timber, although the wind howled overhead. The trees caught most of the snow, and it was not so cold in the aisles of the forest. At the first intersection, where three of the dim trails came together, The Kid stopped to read the signs in the path.

The Spider had hesitated here; had stopped and pondered, as the nervous actions of his horse had resulted in much tramping of the ground, thus telling the story. One of the trails converging here led up the ridge to the right; another led straight ahead; the third turned down to the left. The Kid noted with another glow of satisfaction that The Spider had taken the trail down to the left.

For three hours he followed the telltale imprints of the hoofs of The Spider's horse. They led ever downward, except when the trails he selected led over ridges which promised short cuts. This whole section of the hills was a network of trails which had been made by cattle ranging in the reserve.

It was nearing the early twilight when The Kid finally caught sight of The Spider topping a ridge some distance below him. It would grow dark quickly because of the storm. The Kid abandoned his cautious pace and hurried after the gun fighter. Already he could see the lights of the Jericho to the south.

The Spider saw him coming at the top of the next rise and sent the black plunging down a steep slope. The Kid's gun was in his hand, as he gave chase. If The Spider had not known who he was at first, he most certainly knew by now. Also he must know that he was approaching Jerome, for even a one-time visitor could readily perceive the more prominent of the landmarks.

As he rode, The Kid wondered again why The Spider had not invited a fair gun play on the flats. What was his plan, now that he knew he was again going into Jerome? Did he depend upon Plank and Duffy and their hired ruffians to protect him from a posse? Did he suspect that there was no posse after him because the only pursuer he had seen was The Kid? Would he deliberately resume his role as a bullying gunman and try to make it stick? Or, after all, was The Spider afraid of him?

The Kid did not doubt but that many believed what The Spider had said of him and Burkin—that they were stool pigeons. It was only in such a way, The Kid felt, that The Spider could hope for sentiment on his side.

When The Kid saw how the gun fighter was punishing his magnificent mount, he ground his teeth. Then, as darkness settled down, and The Spider spurred the black down the last treacherous slope above the timber on the ridge north of Jerome, The Kid realized that the gunman was the kind of man who would kill his own horse to further his ends, or save his own skin!

Ten minutes later The Kid entered the west end of Jerome. He saw a light shining in a window of Dad Burkin's cabin, but he didn't go up. He continued on down to the barn in the rear of the hotel. There he found the stableman working over the big black in a stall. The horse was down.

"That measly rat!" the man exclaimed. "He's 'most killed a horse like that."

Dismounting, The Kid left his horse and hurried around to the front of the hotel and met Ed Mately riding in.

"Didn't get a sight of him," growled the deputy.

"He's back here in town," said The Kid quickly. "I ran onto him up north. The blizzard broke on the flats and drove him back. He tried to shoot me from behind. I wonder, did you stop at Dad's place?"

"Burkin ain't dead yet," said Mately. "An' I heard up there that Plank had opened things full blast again because the storm'll keep Curt Donald in the Basin, an' this is pay day at the Jericho."

"Then it's Plank's place for us, Mately," said The Kid grimly. "We want The Spider!"

CHAPTER XXIV
THE DENOUNCEMENT

Mately's information proved to be the truth. Plank's place was ablaze with light and humming with activity. All the card games were going, and the dice tables and roulette wheel were in operation. Blackjack was being dealt, and the white liquor was once more in evidence.

Secure in the knowledge that Curt Donald would not leave the Basin during the storm, and scornful of any effort on the part of Mately to enforce the undersheriff's mandate, Plank and Duffy had reopened after remaining closed for less than twenty-four hours.

Work on the construction of the mill at the Jericho had been suspended at noon because of the storm. Most of the workers employed in putting up the big, new building had been working outside, and the weather had halted their labors. As a result, the workers had flocked into town in a body. The company had paid off for the week at noon. All the men had money in their pockets, and Plank and Duffy smiled smugly, as they began to take their harvest.

Let this day pass, and the authorities could take any action they wished, for Plank and Duffy and their associates would have cleaned up enough to permit them to close down with a fortune. A roar of approval had gone up all over the camp when it became known that Plank's place and the other resorts had "thrown the lid away."

193

The men had been incensed at Donald for ordering the games shut down. Plank had seen to it that such a false impression was created that the men actually thought they had been imposed upon. They felt grateful toward Plank and Duffy for braving the consequences to see that they, the men, as Plank explained cunningly, "got a square deal."

All the men in the camp who were awaiting the completion of the mill before their time for work would come again, joined with the construction crew in an orgy of gambling and drinking. It was a night of storm—a good night to be inside. The big stove in Plank's place was glowing red, and the room was overly warm, scented with sweating bodies, with steaming clothing, with tobacco smoke and reeking fumes of the vile white liquor. The place was in an uproar.

Such was the scene when The Kid, his eyes narrowed and jaw set, and Mately, white-faced, but duty-bound to see it through, entered to the jeers of a score of men grouped about the upper end of the bar. The Kid's quick glance sought every man in the place, and he frowned in disappointment. The Spider was not there. Perhaps he had stopped somewhere to eat. Either that, or Plank's crowd were hiding him.

Plank saw them as soon as they came through the door. His face darkened, and he strode angrily toward them.

"You're blacklisted here!" he cried to The Kid. "You better beat it while the beating is good. I'm telling you for your own good. This ain't no hang-out for stool pigeons!"

Men on all sides muttered, and The Kid saw dark looks directed at him. He saw Duffy, dealing cards at a table, cease his labors with a sneering grin.

All at once the disgusting nature of the scene and what it portended, was brought home to him. The place where Dad Burkin's faro layout had been was now occupied by a table where blackjack was being dealt. In a flash The Kid thought of Fred Renault, who had been unfairly killed in this very place, and of Dad Burkin, who had been shot down here. Gamblers, both of them; but gamblers of a different school, representing different principles—principles as foreign to a man of Plank's stamp as anything could possibly be. When his eyes sought Plank's, they blazed with contempt.

"Plank, you're just naturally low," he said in a loud, clear voice. "I never got hep to just how low you are till this minute. I see now that it was you who was responsible for Fred Renault getting killed in here, even if you wasn't there when it happened. An' you're the one that's to blame for Dad Burkin getting shot. Now you're tryin' to bluff it through by takin' advantage of Mately here, when Curt Donald's away. You ain't got sense enough to see that you can't bluff the law with the people of this county behind it!"

Plank's face had purpled. "The law?" he yelled in a frenzy of rage. "Who's the law? Since when have *you* been talkin' law? Ain't you killed two men out an' out? Now, because you ain't in on the play, maybe, you an' that poor stick of a deputy behind you want to cut these men out of their rights!"

Several men had edged up behind Plank, and The Kid recognized the signs. He took a step backward, and his gun leaped into his hand.

"Plank, if you want a wild town like you say, tell your men to start something!"

Every man in the place looked at the menacing attitude of The Kid and knew he meant it.

"You've told these men a lot of pure bunk," The Kid continued, speaking to Plank, but keeping his darting gaze on all in the room. "Now I'm goin' to tell 'em the truth!"

He snapped a chair around with a whirl of his left arm and leaped upon it. A yell of derision from several of the men died away when a huge, red-haired giant strode out from the bar and shouted to them to desist.

"Let's hear what he has to say," he shouted in a commanding voice that was instantly obeyed.

"Listen to me," cried The Kid in ringing tones. "This is my country—I live here. I was brought up by one of the hardest-shooting an' squarest gamblers that ever put his legs under a table. He was killed right here by a friend of this man Plank, a man who was afraid to meet him in fair gun play. Dad Burkin's another. He never did a wrong turn to a man in his life, an' you all know what happened to him. This Plank called me a stool pigeon, an' I told him to his face he lied. You men know when a man's talkin' truth an' talkin' it straight. That's what I'm giving you now when I whisper that this outfit is just the same as stealing your money at their crooked games."

With an inarticulate yell of rage Plank started forward. Mately, his face white as chalk, stopped him with his gun against his breast.

"Wait till he's through," he cautioned. And Plank, staring out of bloodshot eyes, saw to his amazement that Mately was in deadly earnest.

"I'm not an angel," The Kid's voice rang; "an' I'm not against card games or an open town. I've lived in open towns ever since I can remember. But I'm against plain, every-day robbery by a man, or a bunch of men who want to make you think they're doing you a favor by breaking you clean as a whistle an' making you like it. That's what Plank's doing, an' what Duffy's doing. If you don't believe me look at Duffy's cards; look under the table in the slot he's sitting in—search him!"

There was a roar of voices. Men were getting up from tables. Duffy's face went white at the audacity of The Kid's accusation. The bartender hastily gathered in the filled glasses of white liquor. It was not a time to foment already aroused passions with this villainous liquor.

The Kid pointed with his gun at Plank. "You started it," he cried. "You started it a long time ago, an' you thought you owned these hills an' the men in 'em. You can't stack the cards when you're playin' a game with lies for checks. You're done in these hills, Plank, an' your gun toters an' boosters are goin' with you. You called me something I'm not an' never was, an' I'm going to show these men *why* you wanted 'em to think that about me an' about Dad Burkin!"

He turned to survey the room with flashing eyes. "Take a good look at Duffy's table," he shouted. "Rip that roulette wheel off its hinges an' see the works. Then, if you want to go on playing—go to it!"

The red-haired giant pushed his way to the roulette wheel and, gripping it in his huge hands, tore it from the table. Several fine wires were disclosed. Their function for controlling the wheel was all too obvious. The place was in a turmoil, as the giant cleared a way to Duffy, who had risen, flinging his deck of cards toward the ceiling. The big man grasped his arm, just as he was in the act of pulling his gun. The gun fell to the floor, and the giant picked the gambler up and threw him crashing upon another table. Then he overturned Duffy's table and exposed to view a mechanical hold-out device under the edge of the slot.

"Plank, I'm 'Red' McCarthy, construction foreman for the Jericho. I thought these men were working for me, but I see they were working for you. Boys, I'm boss up on the hill, but I'm not responsible for you down here."

Tables and chairs were overturned, as the men grabbed for the money in the check racks and drawers of the various tables where games had been conducted. Plank, moisture starting out upon his forehead, pushed aside from Mately's gun and rushed for the door, just as it swung open. Mately pulled a chair close to The Kid's and climbed upon it.

"Give it to him!" screamed Plank to the man who had entered.

Both The Kid and Mately turned. Mately lost his balance and swayed behind The Kid, as a shot rang out from the doorway. The deputy fell forward to the floor, and The Kid's bullets sped through the opening into the night.

"The Spider!" some one exclaimed in the sudden hush of voices.

The Kid got down from his chair and bent over Mately, while a man slammed shut the door through which The Spider had retreated immediately after his shot, followed by Plank.

The Kid rose, white-faced. He held Mately's star of authority in his hand.

"Men," he said soberly, "the reason Curt Donald was up to see me was to offer me a job as deputy. I turned it down. Now they've killed Mately, tryin' to get me. I'm taking Mately's place!"

He calmly affixed the star to his shirt. There was a chorus of cheers which speedily gave way to yells of indignation. Some one threw a bottle against the mirror behind the bar, shattering it into fragments and long unsightly cracks. There followed a fusillade of missiles directed at the remaining pieces of mirror and the bottles and glasses on the back bar. Then came the crash of a shattered hanging lamp overhead and burning oil dripped a stream of fire on the floor.

CHAPTER XXV
THE MEETING

The din inside the resort became fearsome, as the frenzied miners and construction workers, infuriated now that they knew how they had been robbed by Plank and his associates, proceeded to wreck the place, while the pungent odor of smoke filled the room.

Men leaped behind the bar, as the men in charge escaped hurriedly through the rear door. Bottles and jugs were smashed or carried away. The cash register was gutted, and several men tried in vain to open the safe in Plank's private office. The lunch counter in the rear was spared, as the restaurant man had given good value for the sensible prices he charged. Some of the men helped him carry away his limited stock to safety outside the building.

Tables and chairs were reduced to kindling wood. Cards and checks were scattered on the floor and hurled into the air by the handful. Pictures and lithographs were torn from the walls, and Plank's desk was overturned, some of the men carrying out account books and packages of papers and letters. The Kid was powerless to stop the destruction. Only for one fleeting moment did he try to halt the work of the maddened dupes of the gambling combine. Then the flames on the floor leaped to tables and chairs and splinters and caught along the bottom of the bar. The smoke rolled upon the men who scrambled madly for the exits, smashing the remaining lamps. In two minutes more the inside of Plank's place was a mass of roaring flame.

The Kid carried Mately's body outside and up the street to the dead deputy's little office. When he returned the flames were bursting from the windows and licking at the roof. In the street pandemonium was at its height. The proprietors of the few other resorts had hurriedly closed when the news was brought to them by breathless messengers. Patrons filed out, thinking the hand of the law was again upon the town. When they learned the truth they were for firing every resort in the place.

It was the giant, McCarthy, and The Kid who brought them to their senses by shouting at the top of their voices that, with the strong wind which was blowing, to fire other buildings might result in burning the town, thus destroying the homes and business places of innocent persons.

Plank's place, situated at the extreme eastern end of the street, was some distance from any other building. The fire there did not endanger the rest of the town. The angry mob surrounded it. Scores of bottles and jugs filled with white liquor—Plank's own product which now was turned against him—were passed about.

In the road beyond the eastern edge of Jerome, just beyond the glare of the flames, three figures were standing. Plank and Duffy were shivering with cold and passion. The third, a small, dark man, whose eye gleamed with the brightness of the burning resort, crouched and stared toward the street and the grotesque scene lit up by the shooting flare of the fire.

Plank was hurling imprecations at the gunman. "You ran away!" he croaked in a querulous voice. "You let him go when you had him in the blizzard, an' when you was drove back here you hid out an' then missed him again. That's all your fault!" Plank pointed a shaking arm at the blazing building.

The Spider looked at him queerly. "I wasn't taking chances of letting him get close enough to pot me in the blizzard," he said in a voice unusually quiet. "I ain't trusting *no* man to shoot square. An' I didn't know I'd hit that fool deputy in there till Duffy come stumbling this way with the word."

"You know what they'll say?" cried Plank hoarsely. "They'll say you was afraid to meet him. They'll say you're yellow, an', s'help me, I believe you are! The yellow Spider—the—"

Plank's words were cut off short, as the butt of The Spider's gun crashed against his mouth, knocking in his teeth and sending him to the ground. Duffy edged away, cowed by the little man's savage expression. The Spider, his eyes glowing like living coals between lids narrowed to mere slits, strode forward. No gunman who has proved his prowess can risk being called a coward. To avoid this meeting would mean that The Spider would carry the stigma with him to his grave. More important, as he well knew, it would mean the gradual losing of his nerve, for the lightning draw is second to the thought that precedes it.

The Kid, standing with McCarthy and a small group of officials from the mine and business men, noted with surprise that the noise of the mob gradually subsided. A hatless miner, flushed with excitement, came running up to them. He looked straight at The Kid, as he fought to recover his breath.

"The Spider's coming!" he blurted.

The Kid made no comment. Already the throng in the street was parting, making way for the gunman, breathlessly eager for more excitement. The crackling of the flames could be heard distinctly. The Kid was smiling faintly. He had not searched for The Spider in the confusion. He had known one of two things would happen: Either The Spider would come to him, in which event he would have to meet him; or the man would endeavor to escape, in which case the arm of the law would reach out for him. Now the meeting was unavoidable.

He walked slowly forward, away from the little group. He could see The Spider between the line of spectators on one side of the street and the burning building on the other. The roof of the building fell in with showers of sparks and a blaze of flame which lit up the scene, until every face and object could be seen distinctly. He walked slightly to the left, so the glare of the flames and the sudden bursts of sparks would not be in his eyes. The light from the fire shone on the star pinned to his shirt. He kept his eyes on The Spider's.

They were barely thirty feet apart, and still The Spider came on. His eyes were flickering with a deadly look of intense hatred, and his lips were curled back against his teeth. He walked catlike. The distance between the two was cut down to twenty feet. The Kid halted. The Spider kept on, his right hand hovering about the butt of his gun. His step quickened. Then his body seemed to shrivel up in an instant, and in that instant came the crack of guns. The Spider stumbled back, firing again. He dropped upon his knees, still firing, as The Kid leaped aside. Then The Spider sprawled in the soft mud of the street and lay still. The Kid dropped his smoking gun and turned away. A wall of what had been Plank's place fell in with a mighty shower of sparks which roared up into the night sky.

CHAPTER XXVI
"TOO ORNERY TO DIE"

Dad Burkin, white and thin, sat in bed propped up against the pillows. In the little bedroom of the cabin were Charley French, Curt Donald, John Reynolds, Lettie, and the doctor.

"I'm beginning to think you'll pull through," said the doctor with a smile.

"Doc, I reckon I'm too ornery to die," said the old gambler. "Anyway, I'm not going to pass out till I see that young fellow over there married and settled down." He frowned at The Kid, who smiled at the blushing girl beside him.

"I was just thinking, Dad, that you might be up an' around by Thanksgiving, an' that that might be a better day to get married on than Christmas," said the boy.

"Why, say," exclaimed John Reynolds, "if you wait till Christmas there'll be so much snow in the hills that we won't get back over Milestone to home!"

"Now, father," protested the girl, "we can't move Mr. Burkin for two months yet. Can we, doctor?"

"Move me? What's that got to do with it?" asked Burkin.

The Kid hitched his chair nearer the bed and took one of the old gambler's hands in his.

"You're coming to live with us, Dad," he said earnestly. "We're going to build a big new cabin over on Tenderfoot, with a room in it for you. You can ride around the place on that big black horse of yours and take it easy. That's what we all want."

"Me become a hill farmer?" said Burkin, trying to glare. "And that horse The Spider had—I'm going to give him to Lettie for a wedding present. No, I reckon I've got to stay in town. But I might take a trip back East to see that girl of mine who's in school back there."

The doctor rose to leave. "You don't need any more medicine," he laughed. "I'll have to begin to give you sedatives instead of stimulants."

"We're not goin' to be farmers, Dad," declared The Kid. "We're going to raise stock. Even Curt Donald here says that's a good business, since I gave up my deputy job. An' there's nothing for you here in town now. Plank's place is gone, and the other resorts have seen the light of reason since the election which put the sheriff in again stronger than ever. You might as well settle down with us on Tenderfoot. You can get East from there as well as here. An' if you want to see Lettie an' me married, that's where you'll have to come, because that's where the preacher is goin' to perform. That's final."

"Well, we'll see," said Burkin. "It ain't wise to give in to you young folks too easy. I'll have to draw cards maybe, and I might get a better hand."

"No, Mr. Burkin," laughed the girl, "you can't draw cards any more, because you said yourself you'd never gamble again."

"Then I guess I might as well go to Tenderfoot," sighed the old man.

Curt Donald took his leave that afternoon. He had made two trips to Jerome in the weeks which had passed since the burning of Plank's place and the demise of The Spider. He had reached the town the day after the gun duel and had recognized The Spider as being a man who was wanted for murder and robbery. The Kid had retained his post as deputy until another man could be appointed.

Plank and Duffy had succeeded in keeping hidden until other members of the combine had searched for the safe in the debris left by the fire and had returned with the information that the safe had been taken to the Jericho by the miners and construction workers. The members of the combine had followed Plank and Duffy out of the country, without demanding the return of the safe or its contents.

Indian summer had arrived on the heels of the blizzard, and the work on the Jericho mine buildings was nearly completed. The company had announced development on a high scale, and other companies had decided that, with the improvement in conditions in the town, they would open their properties and prospect new ones. Jerome faced a new and permanent boom.

The men who had got back a large share of their losses at Plank's tables, tried to make The Kid a gift, but he refused it. As a fair division was impossible, the money was placed in an emergency fund for disabled workers of the Jericho.

Thus it came about that on a day toward the end of the short Indian summer a great throng of men gathered on the slope below the Burkin cabin and walked behind The Kid, Lettie Reynolds, her father, and Dad Burkin, as they rode toward the pass on Milestone.

The girl reined her horse close to The Kid's and took his hand, as the cheers from scores of throats drifted up to them on the crest of the high ridge across from the Jericho.

Robert J. Horton was born in Coudersport, Pennsylvania in 1889. As a very young man he traveled extensively in the American West, working for newspapers. For several years he was sports editor for the *Great Falls Tribune* in Great Falls, Montana. He began writing Western fiction for Munsey's *All-Story Weekly* magazine before becoming a regular contributor to Street & Smith's *Western Story Magazine*. By the mid 1920s, Horton was one of three authors to whom Street & Smith paid 5¢ a word—the other two being Frederick Faust, perhaps better known as Max Brand, and Robert Ormond Case. Many of Horton's serials for Street & Smith's *Western Story Magazine* were subsequently brought out as books by Chelsea House, Street & Smith's book publishing company. Although all of Horton's stories appeared under his byline in the magazine, for their book editions Chelsea House published them either as by **Robert J. Horton** or by **James Roberts**. Sometimes, as was the case with *Rovin' Redden* (Chelsea House, 1925) by James Roberts, a book would consist of three short novels that were editorially joined to form a "novel". Other times the stories were magazine serials published in book form, such as *Whispering Cañon* (Chelsea House, 1925) by James Roberts or *The Prairie Shrine* (Chelsea House, 1924) by Robert J. Horton. It may be obvious that Chelsea House, doing a number of books a year by the same author, thought it a prudent marketing strategy to give the author more than one name. Horton's Western stories are concerned most of all with character, and it is the characters that drive the plots rather than the other way around. He died of bronchial pneumonia in 1934 at the relatively early age of forty-four. Several of his novels, after Street & Smith abandoned Chelsea House, were published only in British editions, and Robert J. Horton was not to appear at all in paperback until quite recently.